Back 2 Life

By

Greg L. Johnson

Marvell Monroe Simmons- Stay strong and I'll see you soon.

Darmino Raymondo Bonds- May he rest in peace.

Gregory Leon Johnson Jr. & Amar Christyan-Samuel Johnson- If you believe, you can achieve.

Table of Contents

ME & MY CREW

It was the 26th of June in the year 1991. The day started off just as any other typical Bay Area day. I woke up at about 10:30 A.M. (the usual). It was just in time to see the rays of sunlight sneaking through the clouds. This let me know a couple of things right off the bat. It was probably going to be between 70 and 80 degrees for the day, and I had a choice to make. Before I strike out and do my thing I could put on pants and a long sleeve shirt and suffer for a couple of hours before the night falls and be out of the house without a return trip, or I could put on shorts and a short sleeve shirt and after a couple of hours kickin' it at Shea's house, before the night falls and the Bay Area breeze kicks in, I'd have to make a trip back to the house to change.

In the middle of this thought the phone rings. "Hell – la," I answer. "What's crackin'' – boy?", says the voice on the other end. It was none other than D – luv. Darrell Ray was his given name. D and I made up half of the foursome I like to call "my crew." I told D I was just thinking of what to wear for the day and waking my ass the hell up. He asks "What time are you going to Shea's house today?" I replied, "About 1 or 2 o'clock, depending on how much T.V. I was gonna watch and what mom's wanted me to do around the house." He said he would probably be through at about 3:00 or 3:30 and he would see me there. I was like, "Alright then," and we hung-up.

Before I could get off of the phone good, it rings again. I answer, "Hell-la." The deep raspy voice on the other line says, "What's up?" It was my potna T-BO, Terrence Bronson. He was known as the muscle of the crew. I was like, "What's crackin'' nigga?" He told he had just got through working out and he was about to go running. I was like, "Damn, you do more before 12 o'clock than most niggas do all day." He replied, "Fuck you nigga, what time are you going to Shea's?" I told him, "About 1 or 2." He was like, "Cool, I'll be there about 2:30 PM."

I was like, "Remember you got the fortys for the day." He replied, "I know, I know, I'll holla when I get there." And with that, the conversation ended. Now I finally get the chance to go to the bathroom and drain last night's alcohol. There is nothing quite like taking that first piss of the day. It's long enough to gather your morning thoughts and short enough that you could stay moving without falling back into that sleepy spell you just got out of. Just as I finish in the bathroom, the phone rings again. This time it's Shea Jackson. Of course he wants to know what time I'm coming through to his crib, and I tell him at about 1 or 2 o'clock, and that the fellas would be over at about the same time and he was like, "Cool."

That was the extent of our conversation and we hung up. Around this time I heard my name being yelled from downstairs. "William!, William!" I was like, "Yes mom." She said, "Come here, boy." Wiping my face and rubbing my hair, I manage to fumble my way down the stairs. "Huh?" I ask my mom. "What are you gonna be doing today?" she asked. "I don't know. I'll probably go kick it at Shea's," I reply. She says, "You know you can't kick it at Shea's forever don't you? Eventually you will need to get a job." I reply, "I know mom, I just want to kick it for a while before I go to college instead of work." Her response was, "O.K., boy. Don't make this a habit. I won't be having any of that in my house and neither is our dad." I gave her an "O.K. moms," and I was back upstairs. My moms would give me the responsibility speech every so often so I wouldn't wind up like my uncles. All three of them wound up getting caught up in drugs and alcohol when I was young, and she didn't want me going that route. Believe me, this is something my mom didn't have to worry about. I didn't know exactly what I wanted to be when I grew up, but I knew I wasn't going that route. Between watching episodes of the Twilight Zone and Perry Mason I hit a couple of sets of push-ups and sit-ups.

I finally decided to go with the pants and the long-sleeved shirt with a tank top underneath, in case it got too hot. I could take off my long sleeve shirt and show off my arms fresh off the push-ups. So I pick out my pants and shirt, get showered and cologned up and get ready to walk to Shea's.

Shea was only a fifteen-minute walk away from me. I liked walking to his house because it always gave me time to reflect on things. As I would walk down the train tracks, I would sometimes think about what I wanted to do in the future, other times I would just think about life in general. You know the usual things like, Why are we here? Where do you go when you die?, and things of that nature. I think it's important to dig in your mind from time to time and ask these questions. And before you know it, "ding-dong". I could see a short, muscular figure walking towards the door through the thin shades and the door opens to "What up nigga?" I was like, "What's crackin' baby boy?"

During which we exchange pounds. I asked if D or T had been through yet and Shea replied, "Do you see them, nigga?" I had to give him the finger to that reply. I sit down in front of the idiot box and sink into Shea's couch, which had to be the most worn-down bunch of wood, cotton and nylon in all of black America. Meanwhile, Shea was moving busily around the house picking up odds and ends doing some makeshift cleaning of the mess from the night before. I told him, "I don't know why you're cleaning. It's just gonna get messed up all over again today." He replied, "I'll clean it up again after that jackass." I told him, "I'm not gonna be to many more niggas or jackasses, dicknose." But, I know this wasn't true because, we could barely get in three words to one another without uttering some sort of profanity.

In the middle of his cleaning, Shea just blurts out, "You know what this bitch told me last night?" The bitch he is referring to is his main chick, Cynthia. I was like "What?" Then Shea says, "Man she told me I was a hater." I was like, "Damn, why did she say that?" He replied, "Man, we was watching a movie with this chocolate nigga in it who kept licking his lips, and I was like, "He's gay." She was like, "He ain't gay!" I was like, "He gotta be gay. Why a nigga gonna keep lickin' his lips every time he speaks to somebody?" She was like, "He don't lick them every time he speaks to somebody. Only when he talks to women, and some women might think that's sexy."

So I was like, "Oh, do you think that shit is sexy too?" Then she said, "That's why you called him gay." And I was like, "Why?" She replied, "You know you thought he was attractive too, and that's why you asked if I thought he was sexy.", so I just told her to shut the fuck up because if she had the chance she would fuck him and give us both AIDS, because he's bisexual. Then he asks what do I think. I had to give him the best answer I know how and I replied, "I think you're both right."

Shea was like, "Huh?" I replied, "I think he's gay. Plus, you find him sexy and if she had the chance she'd fuck him and all three of you would have that shit." We both laughed and Shea threw me a "Fuck you!"

As Shea gets back to his cleaning the doorbell rings. Shea shouts out, "Who is it?" And the deep, raspy voice bellows back, "It's T!" Shea replies, "It's open, nigga." Through the door comes a big 6'2", 230-pound muscular figure. He came through in his usual apparel: jeans, t-shirt, and tennis shoes. To our delight, he had a big brown paper bag and we could hear the bottles clinking against one another. T-Bo walks over to me and gives me a pound and hands me a forty of Mickey's. I felt the bottle was a little warm and I asked T if he pissed in the bottle, recapped it and decided to give it to me. He replied, "They have been sitting out for a while and might be a little warm.", so I get up and put my beer in the freezer. By this time Shea was putting his in the freezer also.

So from there all the beers went in the freezer. I make my way back to the couch and T sits diagonally to the left of me on the loveseat. Shea makes his way back into the living room and sits on the other end of the couch by me. We all settle in and start watching some television.

Thirty or forty minutes go by and I start towards the freezer to get my forty and the doorbell rings. Since I'm up already, I have to make a quick decision: do I get my forty real quick, which should be nice and cold, or should I turn around and get the door? T makes my decision for me, as if he were in my mind. He goes and gets the door as I continue towards the freezer. At the door was none other than D – Luv. D always has to make an entrance when he comes in anywhere. He doesn't necessarily scream or shout out anything, it's just his swagger when he comes in. It is really infectious throughout our crew, too. We all feel a little more at ease or empowered when he's around. D makes his way around the living room with pounds and "What's crackin'?" to every one and we all return the greeting. With that done, the crew is all here and complete. After his grand entrance, D heads straight towards the freezer as if his beer had a homing device and retrieves his beer and gives Shea and T their beers too. After this everyone is settled in and pacified like babies with milk bottles. As everyone is feeling a little freer we get to tellin' stories about our girls we got, and the extent they go to please us. As usual D always has the best story. This one was a little better than usual through. D starts into his story about this chick he has named Gracie. I met her a couple of times before. She was a tall, light skinned girl standing about 5'11". She looked like she weighed about one hundred sixty or seventy pounds. We call girls in this range Thorodales. She had a mixture of thoroughbred and Clydesdale. I mean, she was bad. She had hair to the middle of her back, a cute little nose (with a nose ring), size thirty eight or forty D's, a pretty-ass face, and always stayed manicured and pedicured up, and had the smartest mouth you ever wanted to hear.

With this said, you get an idea of the girl D's talking about. He sets the scene all the way back to the time she paged him when we were kickin' it the night before., so she pages him at about eleven thirty and that's when he breaks away from us to make a quick phone call. During his conversation with Gracie, I heard D say he wanted to shake hands with Tone, and that was followed by laughter but I paid it no mind because I thought that Tone might have been her man, and it was a private joke between the two of them, but as the story further developed I found out, it was something totally different or then again, maybe not. D continues, he left us at about twelve o'clock and is on his way to meet Gracie. He gets to her sister Aisha's house, where Gracie is spending the night, and Aisha yells out of the window when D is walking up, "You think you gonna get some puddy tonight, don't you boy?" D is like, "Girl, where the hell is your sister?" Aisha responds out of the window, "She's in the bathroom washing her coochie, getting ready."

He said he heard someone yell, "Shut up," in a sheepish voice in the background. He gets to the door and Aisha is there to let him in. He walks in the house through the main hallway, and as he's walking past the corridor to his right he hears Gracie yell from one of the rooms to the right, "Come here." He busts a quick right and he's in another hallway and sees Gracie in the second room on the right. He explains how the room looks in different shades of blue from it being dark and her having the television on. She says to him "Why do you still have your clothes on?" He replies, "Damn, I just came in this mothafucka, can a nigga get comfortable?" To which she answered, "No." D then got into his "Alright then" mode and responded with, "Come here and give me some help." D said she moved out of the position she was sitting in, which was sitting on her butt with her knees to her breast, and her arm around her knees, to quickly going to her knees at the edge of the bed with her big titties just a bouncing. She was fumbling around trying to unbutton, unbuckle, and unzip his pants.

D is drooling as he's telling us this story, which is unusual for him because he's touched quite a few females. So he goes on, "Yeah, she's fumbling on my zipper and then when she gets it unzipped, boom, my hard ass nasty nine is right in her face." He continues, "As soon as she saw it she made this sexy-ass face and whispered, "Ooh wee" in this sexy-ass voice and just started gobblin' like a turkey and I was like, "God damn! I love your mom for giving birth to you." We all fall out laughing at this statement. The laughter goes on for a minute and then D continues. "Man, I had to push her away from me and back onto the bed." He says at this point Gracie was like, "Why did you do that?" To which he replied, "That shit felt too good, so now, it's time for daddy to be up in that ass."

To which Gracie opened her legs as wide as all outdoors and said, "Come get it daddy." At this point I had to hide my wood, because it was getting graphic up in here. I looked at Shea and T and got reassured because they looked just as enamored as I did. At this point D tells us he went to town. In and out, back and forth, up and down for about thirty minutes, at which point he tells her to turn around. He says Gracie was acting reluctant, which made him want it more., so he just flips her over, kind of surprised and turned on by this, she tells D, "Don't get mad" and he just says "Hell, what I got to be mad about?" Then he explains to us how she has a tattoo of a handprint on her ass with the name Tone on the inside of the palm. We were like, "Whoa." D then tells us how he's hittin' it from the back and slapping hands with Tone. At this we had to give a round of applause. This had to be the best one yet. After this and a couple of suds guzzling, dominoes, and television, it was closing in on two in the morning. I was thinking, "Damn where did the day go?" But this was typical for us. We would wake up, hook up at Shea's and see what the day would bring us. Sometimes it would be a little bit of nothing. Sometimes it was a lot of something. Either or, it was all right with us.

D-LUV

As the summer progresses, days get longer and hotter. More often than not, this means the crime rate goes up in urban areas. When it gets hot, niggas just get plain stupid sometimes. For D this wasn't necessarily a bad thing. Dope fiends usually go to deeper lengths to get the money to buy what they need and this means more money for the D-boys. Deep into the month of July this was very good for D because the money was rolling in. D usually had two sets of friends he hung with.

He hung with our crew, which was his square set of friends, and he hung with his cousin young Vell. His given name was Marvell Simmons. Now to us D was big ballin'. But to the world at large young Vell was big ballin'. Vell had the big body Benz, the house on the hill, all the girls you could possibly want, and respect galore. His resume in the streets was very thick and D got props just because he was Vell's blood cousin. Amongst this circle, D-Luv was seen as square. Vell and all his potnas hustled because they had to.

D had a caring mom and a hardworking dad. D's dad was out of town working a lot, so I think the male figure D grew up admiring most was his cousin. Don't get me wrong though: D was far from a punk. He was good from the shoulders when he had to be, but in the dope game how you throw 'em from the shoulders don't matter much when the next coward has an itchy trigger finger. D and Vell were close because when they were little kids D, being a year older, used to stick up for Vell all the time. Now Vell, having earned his rep on the streets, was returning the favor. On this particular hot July day, D was kickin' it with Vell and some of his potnas drinking fortys, smoking bomb and woo-ridin' any and everybody. Vell was ridin' D for being a square and D was right back at him about sticking up for him in the past. Everyone was laughing and having a good time. D noticed down the block there was someone staring and mugging them. Vell was like, "You know who that is, nigga?" D was like "Who?" Vell replied, "That's that ugly, chocolate, gibbons guerilla lookin' ass nigga, Cornelius." Right then, Cornelius stepped more into the sunlight and D was like, "Oh, how could I have not noticed that shiny, shaved down guerilla?" Everyone started laughing and from the way everyone looked in his direction and started laughing, Cornelius knew they were laughing at him.

Cornelius (pronounced Kah-nee-yus) to the cats in the hood was the biggest, blackest dude you ever want to meet. He was 6'4," 245 lbs, without a lick of fat on him. All this dude likes to do was beat people up for their money and basically punk any person he felt was a weak link. He never messed with the D-boys because as much as he could kick most people's ass, he didn't want to die.

Basically it was a sort of sick mutual respect. He didn't mess with the D-boys and they didn't pay him much mind. After the loud laughter in his direction, Cornelius seemed to pay D extra attention when he walked back to his porch. D, who is never to be taken lightly, paid him a little extra attention also. Meanwhile, a dice game breaks out between Vell, D and the rest of the dudes they were kickin' it with. There's about two grand on the pavement and D is breakin' em. Some days things just go like that. D seemed to have more of those days than the rest of us. Pagers continuously go off throughout the game, between friends walking up on the spot, and cats taking trips around the corner to serve dope. But eventually, too much money was being missed by cats hangin' out, so people started going their separate ways to continue their hustle.

D, Vell and another one of Vell's potnas named Nino stayed and hung out a little longer. They were talking about things that were going on in the streets like which girls were hot in the town in more ways than one. Who the up and coming ballers were, who thought they were ballin' but couldn't even dribble, who was washed up in the game and everything else under the sun. It was basically like the neighborhood CNN, up-close and personal. This was how our crew stayed up on that was going down in the streets. D would relay everything that was going on back to us. It seemed as though Vell always made sure to hang out a little every night with his cousin so he could keep well informed. After they finished the bulk of their conversation and the small talk was winding down, a carload of females rolled by.

Vell, being his normal self yells for the girls to stop and come back and holla at him and his potnas. There were three of them in the car, and Vell, D, and Nino hanging. The girls turn around, pull up to the curb and park. The driver looked like Grimace, as usual. The passenger and the girl riding in the back seat looked cool.

Nino, who was also called homo-habalous for his chimp-like features, knew his position and immediately went to the driver. Vell always tried to play big dog in these situations but D was one of those pretty boy gangsters, so he went for his and often got the girl he wanted. Vell started to talk to the passenger but noticed she was looking at his cousin and asked her was she felling his cousin more. She didn't say anything but, it was written all over her face. Vell just turned to D and said, "Cuzzo handle this." After this, Vell jumped onto the breezy in the backseat while D handled the passenger. Everyone was joking and having a good time, talking and laughing. Vell got a page amidst all the laughter and conversation.

The breezy he was talking to asked him, "Why you got a pager, are you a doctor or something?" Knowing she knew why he had a pager, Vell just replied, "Yeah I'm Doctor Feelgood. When people ask they call daddy for medication." You could tell by the look in her face that her panties got wet when she heard him say that. Most females like that fast furious life at one point or another, but when the real shit goes down and they get a taste of what its really like behind the glitz and glamour, that's usually the point when they decide it's time to find a square. Vell asked the female he was talking to if she wanted to take a walk with him around the corner. At first she reacted like he was out of his mind, but with very little urging she agreed to go with him. The driver immediately tried to stop her from leaving, telling her she just met him and she didn't know what he was into, but Nino played his role perfectly and with a little urging of his own talked Grimace (the driver) into joining them on their walk. Vell asked D if he was going to be able to hold it down until he got back, and with no hesitation D replied, "Of course" and off they went to serve one of Vell's local knocks. D was left by the car talking to this girl he just met.

I came to find out later that her name was Marie. She was a tall slender chick. She was half-black and half-Filipino and had hair to the middle of her back. To put it in more familiar terms, she was a traffic stopper. Their conversation consisted of what high school did you go to, oh, you went there? I went to school here. Do you know so and so? and things of that nature. It's obvious that they really dig each other and D is just about to ask her for her number and talk about the next time they'll probably get to see each other, when he hears a deep voice coming from behind him saying, "What's up nigga?" It was none other than Cornelius. D always knew he was a big dude but, to see him up close and personal was something to behold.

Now D wasn't necessarily a short dude, but Cornelius was built like an NFL linebacker. D replied back to him "What's up with you nigga?" Cornelius replied, "You cats seemed to have a lot to laugh at earlier and I want to laugh too. So tell me what was the big joke?" D replied, "Wasn't nothing to it. It was just niggas clownin'." Cornelius snaps back, "Well to tell you the truth, niggas looked like they was laughin' at me, and if that's, so we got a problem." At this point, D had a decision to make. He knew the only reason Cornelius ran up on him was because his cousin and the rest of his homies weren't around.

Whether D liked it or not, he was pretty much the most square dude out of everybody on the block. D was a good fighter from the shoulders but the tales of Cornelius beating people to a pulp were running rampant through his mind. D took a quick peek at the female he was talking to and she had a look in her eyes like, "Nigga what you waiting for?" With that, D just took off. Boom! D went straight to the nose of Cornelius.

This punch was like a donkey kicking an unsuspecting innocent bystander. But Cornelius wasn't an innocent bystander and D damn sure wasn't a donkey. Cornelius, although injured, shocked and utterly embarrassed by getting hit in the nose, was also infuriated by what had just transpired. He stumbles backwards as if he were back-peddling and trying to run forward at the same time. I think back to how D was explaining the situation to me and figured Cornelius must have been thinking, to get hit is one thing, but to fall from that hit is another.

So, Cornelius managed to shake off the blow, while D was just standing there basking in the glow of what he thought he had just accomplished. Before he even got the chance to pat himself on the back, Cornelius was back to standing and looking like D just robbed him for all the bananas in the western block of the jungle. Cornelius seemed to get on all fours for a milli-second and got close enough on D to stand on his hind legs and "ba-boom!" Two blows, that quickly. He hit D with a left jab, just to get D's face in place to line up with a right power punch. D fell to the ground quickly, but unlike most of Cornelius victims, D didn't stay down too long. So now Cornelius, standing there in the middle of his basking in the glory of what he thought he had just did and was utterly shocked to see D rise to his feet. It wasn't like D just hopped up after the blow, but he got up in enough time to have

Cornelius thinking twice about what he might've gotten himself into. Meanwhile, a couple of neighbors standing around take notice to what has transpired.

The girl D was talking to seem to be mesmerized about seeing some real gangster shit going down. She backed up just enough to let the action take place, without being in harm's way, but close enough to tell all of her friends the details. Now they stood toe to toe. Cornelius was not rushing in on D to take him out quick. And D, hoping desperately for any kind of opening to get another clean hit. With no warning, Cornelius bounces like a big silverback on D. They are struggling all over the concrete and Cornelius' momentum has him with the obvious advantage.

Whether it was out of fear or the real soldier in D, he put up a working man's effort that day. He brought his hard-hat and his lunch to work. On the sidelines, Marie was already sold. If D could make it out of this battle alive, he was going to get the time of his life. I didn't know D carried a pistol the majority of times we were together, but I guess it was meant for him to have one that faithful day.

Without even thinking of what he was doing, D was struggling to stay out of position for Cornelius to get a good hold of him. He reached for his deuce-deuce in his right sock. Yes, his right sock. I know this sounds funny, but I know that when D did have his gun, he always kept it in his right sock, with the elastic out, and the gun being kept in place by two

thick, tight yellow rubber bands. Somehow, D was able to get a hold of the gun, and a shot went off. The onlookers quickly ran in their houses.

Marie was in the open, too much in the clear to be worried about ducking for cover. Besides, she was still far enough away to feel like she wasn't in harm's way. No one was hit. It did cause Cornelius to get off of D. It gave D time to stumble back and gather himself to get to his feet. Now we have a stand-off of a different kind. Cornelius is the one who has doubt in his mind and D is standing proud. D has convinced himself that Cornelius will bow down and accept this battle as a draw and give D his respect. But some people are just plain hard-headed.

Often times we start to believe in the way people perceive us so much, that we unknowingly become just that: what people perceive us as. With this said, Cornelius gives it one more guerilla charge and D has yet another choice to make: Are you a killa in this game or pretender in this game? Marie closes her eyes because the situation has gotten too real for her. Cornelius closes his eyes during the charge. D closes his eyes and lets off two shots.

Pop! Pop! Right when the shots are going off, Vell, Nino and the two breezyd were hitting the block. Cornelius' momentum once again leads him to land on top of D, this time his body is motionless. D is in shock, with this big, heavy body laying soulless on top of him. He slowly shrugs Cornelius' body to the left of him. Vell and Nino run up to make sure D is O.K.

D is in shock at the moment and not very coherent. Vell grabs the gun from D and yells at the girls to take his cousin home while he tries to clean the crime scene. At first there is confusion, but Vell yells, "Take my cousin home, bitches!" Marie immediately shoves D in the backseat. D couldn't take his eyes off of the soul he had taken from earth. Vell and Nino stay behind to pick up anything D might've left behind and cleaned out Cornelius' pockets while they were there. Cornelius' pockets were empty, as they had expected; there was no money to be found on his body. But in digging deeper into Cornelius' pockets, Vell found a picture.

It was a picture of his mom with Cornelius when he was a baby. All of a sudden, instead of being some wild animal that Vell thought should be put to sleep, he became a momma's son and a living, breathing human soul. But rules in this game are very cold. If you choose to dip and dab in the underworld, it tends to label you a fan of the game instead of a participant, and if you are a fan of the game you are not a true player. Thus, your cards get dealt accordingly., so for Vell, Cornelius was nothing more than the background to his painted picture. Vell took the picture, the gun, and D's wallet that fell out of his pocket during the struggle and got the hell out of dodge.

D was on the way home, and Marie decided it wasn't safe for D to go home. They stopped at a phone booth and D called his parents and told them he was spending the night at my house. His pops said it was all good and Marie guided D back to the car, and told him he was sneaking into her house tonight and spending the night.

D was still in shock at this time and feeling numb to the world. D's pager is going off like crazy and Marie takes it and puts it in her purse. As they got off of the freeway and drove for miles into the boonies, they finally come upon a suburban community. Marie's parents had big bread and lived thirty minutes from hell, but it looked so heavenly.

They pulled up to the house and Marie's potnas were like, "Take care girl, and don't do nothing we wouldn't do." Marie just helps D out of the car and looks at her girls like, "Fuck ya'll." The car pulls off and Marie directs D to a window about waist-high and near a well-groomed bush. D goes to the window, while Marie goes around to the front of the house. The house was a creamy pink color, shaped in a horseshoe fashion with a statue of a Greek Goddess in the middle of a circular driveway. D wasn't actually tripping off of the magnitude of money that house must've cost. But instead, his mind was on a dead body. Marie turns on a light and heads towards the window to let D in. Once inside D takes a look around and starts to realize, "O.K., I'm not at home. What the hell am I doing here?" Sensing this, Marie quickly turns off the light and tells D to undress. His pager keeps going off. Marie pulls it out of her purse and looks at the number with a 911 at the end of it. Marie calls the number. "Hello!" Vell yells into the phone. Marie replies, "Hello?" "Where is my cousin?" Vell replies. "He's about to get his boots knocked, if you know what I mean," Marie says.

Vell answers, "Let me holla at him." Marie tells D it's his cousin on the phone and tells Vell to make it quick. Marie holds the phone to D's ear and D says, "Hello." Marie quickly pulls the phone back and says to Vell, "See, he's O.K. I'll drop him off at home in the morning, O.K.?" Vell says, "O.K., take care of my cousin." And they hung up. Marie looks at D and says, "Are you ready?" D asks, "Ready for what?" Marie says "Ready for this." She takes off her clothes and stands in the middle of the room. D says, "Hell yeah." And that night, a star was born.

KICKIN' IT

Although it was summer, there was still something special about Saturday nights. T, Shea and I decided we would go catch a horror flick and then go kick it on Telegraph Ave. You see, besides being known for having weirdoes hang out at people's park, Berkeley was also known as the hang out spot on Saturday nights. We would go there and get a slice of Blonde's pizza and a coke for a dollar fifty and just hang out.

From time to time we might pick up a couple of albums, because T liked to deejay in his spare time, but most of all we liked to look at the ladies. We all had our main chicks but hey, at eighteen or nineteen one could never have enough. We decided to go check out *Nightmare on Elm Street*. We all had a sick sense of humor, so we figured Freddy would make us laugh until our stomachs hurt. And it's always a little easier to laugh after some good California green bud and a forty.

It was especially cool to see T-Bo high. He didn't smoke much because he was always trying to stay in great shape for football, but on occasion he would indulge. Shea, on the other hand, was always high or drinking these days. We didn't pay too much attention to this, because it was more like a joke at the time. Little did we know what effect it would take on his life later, but for now it was all fun and games. We always were a little louder than the average moviegoer but it didn't seem fun without some kind of commentary. The key is too know how much commentary is too much commentary.

Me and T were always sliding in a little joke or two, but Shea would want to run down paragraphs to the point we would have to tell him to shut the hell up. We would always find ourselves saying, "A nigga wouldn't do this," or "Only a white boy or girl would do this or that," and things of that nature. It made us think, if black people were in horror movies it would only be ten or fifteen minutes long because the niggas would either run away or shoot the killer. Our high started wearing off, and the screen eventually mesmerized us and pretty soon it began watching us instead of us watching it. Towards the end of the movie, I looked to my left and saw Shea dosing off and to my right T was engrossed in the movie. Myself, I would always watch a movie until the end if I paid good money. The movie eventually ended and I had to slap Shea on his head to wake him up before the lights came on and he looked stupid. He got mad as usual but hey, it was all in a day's work.

We saw a couple of people we knew in the lobby of the movie theatre, and we stopped to talk about what's going on around the bay. It seems as though everybody was talking about D. D was the hottest name in the streets and the streets were talking. This dude we knew named Lemon head was going on talking about how D was a big killer and how he could get any girl he wanted now because he was all the breezys were talking about. He was the big man in the streets. T, Shea and I were like, "Huh?"

We hadn't talk to D for a while because that was just his way. He would come around and kick it hard for a while and he would disappear for a while. We know the routine, but hearing all of this buzzing going around with our boy's name had us tweekin'. We didn't want to give anyone a clue that we didn't know what Lemon head was talking about, so we just gave head nods and short, vague commentary.

After a little more small talk, we said our goodbyes and told everyone we would see them out and about in the traffic. As we started to leave, Shea, T and I each gave each other the look. You know that look of "What the hell?" T looked at me and said, "What the hell did D do?" I turned back to T and said, "Man, don't jump to conclusions, you know how fools get to talking sometimes. There could be something to it but then again maybe not." Shea always had to chime in out of left field. He said, "You know that nigga got killer in his blood." And as if rehearsed, T and I turned to him at the same time and said, "Shut up!"

We made our way to the streets. It was cool night, with a brisk wind blowing in our faces. This was nothing new for a Bay Area summer night. No matter how hot it got in the day, it usually got pretty cool at night. We put a little pep in our step to get to Shea's car. He had a 1978 Cutlass Supreme.

It was given to him by one of his uncles, who worked on cars a lot. He gave it to Shea as a graduation gift. It was a clean car. It was white, with peanut butter brown interior, complete with rally rims. But, in usual Shea fashion, he would talk bad about his car. The rearview mirror was broke and it had a couple of scratches in the paint. Instead of looking at it like all he had to do was put a couple of dollars in the car, he bad-talked his uncle for not doing it before he gave it to him. But, again, this was nothing new. It was only Shea being Shea.

So we're riding. Making our way through the streets, on our way to Telegraph so we could see if there were any breezys walking, so we could start yelling out the window in between sips of our beers. We really weren't yelling anything in particular, but if anyone looked like they were in the least bit interested, we would've pulled over quick. It's funny to see our different styles of trying to talk to the ladies. Myself, well my dad would always tell me, all a girl could say was no. And if you have history with this woman and she turns you down when you ask her for her number, you can't miss what you never had, so you're actually not missing out on anything. Well, maybe a little pride, but hell, shit happens. And who knows, she might say yes. T was what I called the exhibitionist.

He liked the breezy to get a good look at his body. His whole game plan was "If we're driving, you guys holla at the ladies and when you pull over, I'll be the one to get out of the car to show my body for the team." Although, not the most articulate of brothers, T usually said enough to intrigue a woman and get his way into the panties somehow. Another plus for him was, he was going to college to play football. Just as well, as he was going to be on scholarship. Some of these females looked at him as if he was their scholarship. If he could be one of the lucky ones to make it to the pros, it would be like hitting the lotto.

Then there was Shea. Need I say more? Actually, it all depended on what kind of mood he was in. Shea would sometimes come at a woman with respect, until she said that magic word, "Nooooo!" Then, oh my God, it could be like World War III. Females would look at us sometimes like, "I've unleashed the Devil's disregarded, discounted, overlooked Spawn. Can you please help me?" And we would just look at them like "Shit, what the fuck you want me to do? You came to this beast's lair voluntarily." Yes. Shea could be a beast sometimes.

It was funny because a lot of females would make it past the preliminaries, and would make it to the house with Shea. We would come through and kick it. The female would be having a good time with us and then, boom! Someone would crack on Shea, she would start laughing and he would be like, "What you laughing at, bitch?" She would look so innocent and surprised. You know, kind of like that pretty little fawn, when the headlights light their innocent big brown eyes the size of cue balls. Needless to say, that would be the last we saw of her. We didn't get any play before we got to Telegraph anyway, so there was nothing out of the ordinary about this ride.

We finally reached our destination. Parking was very scarce around Telegraph because it was near the UC Berkeley campus, so after we got there it took another twenty minutes just to find parking. We lucked up and saw someone pulling out, so we quickly grabbed their newly-vacated spot. One thing Shea could do well was drive, so it seemed like he would parallel park a car in less than two seconds. After a quick couple of sips of our drink we get out of the car and way towards Blonde's. There were a lot of people out and the scene was buzzing with excitement. I loved to be in an atmosphere like this one, because if nothing else, your soul felt so alive inside. We were clowning with each other all along our walk. Of course, capping on Shea was our usual activity. I was usually the one throwing the most jabs at him and T was always in stitches.

We eventually made our way to Blonde's. The line was all the way out the door, but believe me, this was some pizza worth waiting for. So we got in line and waited just like the rest of the sheep. The line didn't really take too long because most people ordered a slice of cheese pizza or a slice of pepperoni pizza. They always had slices of cheese and pepperoni waiting in the cut. But there was always that specialty prick. You know, that person who would order a sausage, pineapple, bell pepper and extra cheese slice. This would slow the line down but luckily for us, there weren't too many of those. T, Shea and I ordered our usual. Our usual was a slice of cheese pizza and a coke for a buck fifty. None of us were Muslims but, for some reason, we tried to limit our pork intake. Most people who got their pizza took it to go, so there were some empty seats inside. I sprinkled my crushed red peppers and garlic powder on my slice and went to town. I saw a cutie in line peeking at me from time to time., so I tell the fellas, "I'm going to get some napkins." As I make my way to the counter to get the napkins, I just happened to crossed paths with this beautiful young lady. I say "Hello," and she responds the same. I asked her name and she said it was Anitra and I was like, "Damn. That's a beautiful name. My name is Willie, but all my friends call me Willie Wood. So you could call me Willie Wood." She then replied, "Hello Willie Wood."

I knew I had it sewed up from there. I told her me and my friends were out chillin' and asked if she had any friends. Of course I could see she had three friends with her, but it sounded good to ask, so I did. She said, "Yeah, these are my home girls, Sharee, Reina, and Belize." I said,

"Hello," to all of them and looked at my potnas. I gave T and Shea the look. This look was, "Nigga get your asses over here. I got this shit sewn the fuck up." They came immediately. My boys looked like two lions stalking a gazelle with a broken leg. This was both a good and bad situation.

On one hand, we had four beautiful young women who seemed to want to have our company. On the other hand, there was going to be a female without a dude, somehow, someway. I mean when we were going through the friendship and choosing process it was going to be all good for everybody, but oh my God it could get ugly if the variables didn't play out correctly. Everything was going cool, Anitra and I were talking and I could already tell whom my potnas were choosing. T was the type to choose the chocolate brick house, which is what Sharee was. T was talking to everyone but I know this nigga too well. He always gave Sharee an extra couple of looks accompanied with a quick smile. Shea, on the other hand loved anything high yella. His main squeeze Cynthia was a nice caramel complexion but she was the best he could get to be his permanent chick and she really didn't look bad at all. However, his ideal chick was tall, long-haired, and high yella.

I think it was because he had a short man's complex and most niggas think of high yella when they think of beauty. This gave Shea a feeling of supremacy when could get his hands on one of these. Thus, he and Reina were clicking. Reina looked like the type to just fall in where she felt was her position. I don't know it she really was attracted to Shea but she felt he was trying to holla and went with the flow. She was really underachieving this night, but I loved females like this because Shea felt on top of his game and she just wanted to have a good time. As much as I couldn't disagree with my potna's choice in women, I have to say they were sleepin' heavily on their potna Belize. I could see how she lost the sweepstakes because she was a quiet, plain-looking young lady, but if you looked closely you could really spot the beauty underneath the façade. I'm one of those niggas that can spot beauty behind the facade. She looked like plain Jane but damn, she had an exotic undertone to her. You could tell she didn't even know what she possessed but hey, some of us are slower bloomers than others. I wasn't really trippin' because mine looked good. I couldn't see her replacing my main chick Sabrina or nothing, but I saw some good times to be had between us.

We were just walking up and down the streets of Berkeley, on or near Telegraph, when we saw a group of people surrounding a car. We couldn't really tell what was going on because the scene was so thick. As we drew closer to the commotion the people started looking more familiar. The first person we saw that looked familiar was Lemon head. Then the crowd started to part like the Red Sea and all of a sudden D's face appeared. D was leaning on a Fire Red 1991 Acura Legend. We all saw each other at the same time. T, Shea, and I were like, "D, what's up, baby boy?" D replied, "My niggas!" We all gave each other hugs and pounds with a little extra emphasis on affection because we hadn't seen each other in a while, and D seemed to have come up in a major way during his absence from us.

We gave each other the homie look, so we knew not to ask D too many questions about anything right then and there. D's cousin Vell comes out of the crowd looking like a father who was proud of his son. He greeted us all like we were his cousins too. The breezys we were with tried to act like they were upset with us, for ignoring them in front of our homies but, we could tell they liked the high powered status our potna had and the love he showed us rubbed some of that status off on us.

Normally D would've been trying to see what was up with us, and the chicks we were with, especially since there was one too many but, he was busy man today. Everybody was looking at D's car and marveling at his over whelming aura of confidence. We couldn't really talk the way we wanted to, so I told D we would get at him later and catch up on everything. He was like, "Where ya'll going? You trying to dig them breezys out tonight?" The girls heard him and gave him a dirty look but you could tell they really weren't too upset because it was one of those cute dirty looks and not a "Fuck you nigga" look. I was like, "Go on with that nigga." We both laughed because we both knew damn well we were tryin' to dig in these chicks that night, and with that T, Shea and I were on our way with the ladies.

While we were walking, Anitra started asking me all kinds of questions about D, like, "How do you know him?" "Does he sell drugs?", and things of that nature. I was just like, "D is a good guy and a long time friend," and I left it at that. I asked Anitra what her and her friends were going to get into for the night and she said, "I don't know. Do you have any suggestions?" I was like, "Hell yeah! We could go back to my potna Shea's house and kick it." She replied, "What are we gonna do over there?" I said, "We could just play dominos, and have a couple of drinks." She said, "That's cool with me. I have to ask my girls if they're down and if they are we could go from there." I said, "Cool."

I then called Shea and T over for a quick huddle. I told them about what Anitra and I had been discussing and they both looked at me like, "Boy, I could kiss yo ass right now." I told them to hold their tongues so they wouldn't jinx the shit because it all depended on what her home girls were going to say and with there being one more of them than there was of us, anything could happen. Anitra came back, all bubbly and said, "O.K., it's all good as long as you guys have us back at a decent hour," and I replied, "Cool," with a devilish grin. I gave my potnas the look and from there, once again it was on.

From there we walked to the liquor store and I asked Anitra what they were drinking, and she replied, "Gin and juice, of course." T, Shea and I looked at each other like, "Oh, it's going down tonight," so we got some Seagram's gin and some Donald Duck orange juice and piled in Shea's Cutlass. On the way to the house we were all talking about how we were going to whup each other's ass in some dominos and capping on each other back and forth. It was all love between everybody. Shea wasn't getting too far out of pocket. He realized that it was going to be a good time for everybody, so it's like he made a conscious effort to stay his human self tonight and not turn into the volatile half guerilla, half bizarro self he could be sometimes.

T was just on cruise control. He knew it was going down and he rarely would mess up a good thing, so I never worried about T messing anything up. We finally pulled up to Shea's house. We always kicked it at Shea's because his parents weren't together anymore and Shea stayed with his mom and his brother. Luckily for us it was like Shea's mom didn't even live there, because she was always at her boyfriend's and never (and I do mean never) came home. So, basically Shea stayed there with his older brother, Jessie. Jessie was way cool. He would drink and smoke with us from time to time. But tonight we had the house to the neck. Jessie was out of town with some friends of his doing whatever. We really didn't care what, because we just knew he was out of sight and out of mind.

We came in the house and got straight to business. It was like the door opened and I was instantly pouring drinks and shaking up dominos on the table. Since there were seven of us we had two games going on back to back. I was playing with Anitra and Belize, and T and Sharee were playing with Shea and Rheina. I loved my set-up. I was feeling better about myself as the drinks flowed aplenty. Belize started showing me more and more love on the sly. Every time Anitra would get up and go to the bathroom or fix herself a drink, Belize would be talking to me, licking her lips, or touching me in places she shouldn't be touching. If she had bad intentions and by this I mean *bad*, meaning good, I was a willing subject. My daddy told me until I get married the only thing I should turn down is my collar and I listen to my pops religiously. The other girls were getting drunk out of their minds in the meanwhile, and my potnas saw everything in the making. I knew Belize was in the hip pocket, so I focused most of my attention on Anitra. In the meantime, Shea slid upstairs in one room with Rheina. When I saw this happening, I knew it was gonna be a good night.

I knew Shea was taking Rheina to his mom's master bedroom, so I instantly started thinking, "Hmmm… Me, Anitra, Shea's room, sounds like a plan." So I gestured towards Anitra and said, "Oh excuse me" and I took Anitra by the hand, and guided her towards the hallway leading upstairs. There was no resistance at this point in the game. On the way out, I made eye contact with Belize and she looked at me. We both knew I was doing what I had to do right then and there, but at the same time the look on her face suggested, "I'm next" and the look I gave back was, "Don't trip, I got plenty to go around."

So, my plan was implemented. I shot a quick glance at T on my way out, too. He just gave me this funny look and we both laughed at the same time. Now I totally focused my attention on Anitra. I was focusing so much time on Belize that I was losing focus on what I had come up on in the first place. When we were going up the stairs Anitra had this look on her face like "Nigga you done hit the lotto tonight." And to tell the truth, that's how I felt, but for reasons she couldn't fathom.

When we reached the top of the stairs we heard Shea and Sharee in the room getting carnal. Sharee is sounding like Shea is digging in the deepest parts of her orifice and she was screaming at the top of her lungs. I know they can hear her downstairs. And Shea sounds like King Kong beating his chest after conquering New York. It just sounded so wild in there, that my dick got hard just listening. I had to put my ear to the door to get a close up. Anitra quickly grabbed me and was like, "Willie Wood, what the hell are you doing?" I was like, "Shit, my boy is serving that ass up in there and I need to listen for points of reference." She then replied, "You better concentrate on the task at hand before you have to use your hand." And I was like, "O.K." Now I was following her to Shea's room. As soon as we hit the door I pounced on her like a panther.

My tongue was deep down Anitra's throat and she loved it. She started unbuckling my belt buckle and I was under her shirt fumbling with her bra strap. She was having her difficulties and I was having mine. Eventually we just stepped back. I started taking my clothes off and she started taking off hers. We were looking at each other like, "Yeah, motherfucka, your ass is mine." Now we were both butt naked, and it was on.

As soon as I inserted the penis it was total bliss. We were fucking, sucking, licking and sliding everywhere possible. I was on top of my game, so I felt like I was controlling everything. It was passion, lust, raw fucking and everything in between. When I heard Anitra cumming for like the fourth time, I decided it was my time to release. With that we sounded like two cave people howling in the wind. We both physically exhausted each other and instantly fell asleep afterwards. It seemed like eight hours but it was more like twenty minutes later when I woke up and felt thirsty. I slipped into my boxers, while Anitra laid comatose on the bed. I looked at her like, "Yeah, I did that with that" and, I started down the stairs.

I could hear Shea snoring in his momma's room as I passed the door. And when I got to the bottom of the stairs I see T. I couldn't tell if they were asleep or playing possum under the blankets, but I don't care. I'm thirsty and need some water. I go to the kitchen to pour some water and I notice Belize sleeping in the back room on the couch, where we were playing dominos. I'm thinking damn, I'm just through fucking her home girl, so I know she isn't trying to see me like that, so I'm just gonna get my water and go back upstairs. Then I hear a whisper, "Willie, what are you doing down here in your drawls?" I knew damn well she wasn't trippin' off why I was there in my drawls. I was thinking, "What the hell are you doing up? You should be dead asleep," but instead I was like, "Getting some water." Belize then said, "Come here, boy." After I poured my water, I went over to her and said, "What?" She stood up, put my hands on her ass and started kissing me, morning breath and all. In my mind I was thinking, "Damn, my dick is raw and this shit is wrong."

But, on the other hand I was thinking, "Damn, I'm the motherfuckin' man." Belize went one longer than her home girl. She went down and started bossing the wee-wee. I was like "Oh my God, I want to suck your daddy's dick," because this girl was the shit. I was feeling it, so I did the dirty deed. I started licking her cooch like there was no tomorrow. She was my sexual, spiritual partner and I knew it right there. We fucked for a hard thirty minutes. We both came and assumed our positions. She fell back asleep in the back on the couch and I went back upstairs with my water just that quick.

Anitra asked where I was all that time and I told her I was downstairs talking to T. She said, "Oh." And she fell back asleep and we both curled up and fell into the spoon position. The whole house was asleep and everyone was satisfied. We all exchanged numbers in the morning when we took the girls home (and when I say everyone, I mean everyone exchanged numbers), and we had new kick-it potnas. Everything was all good and everyone was happy. After this night, we all had a story to tell. This was just the beginning of more wild nights to come.

DILEMMA

Well, another day, another dollar. As the summer starts to wind down, the days seem to get shorter. It's been a while since I had a talk with my girl Sabrina. She's been busy getting herself ready for college and taking life seriously. On the other hand, I've been kickin it, bullshitting and getting into any and everything I can.

It incenses me sometimes to think about how mature this young lady can be. Sabrina is the one in her clique that always gets hit on by the older, more mature cats. The little young horn dogs around our age tend to stir clear of her. The mature dudes tend to hit on her because she's young and fresh, and they think they could get into her mind because they've been around the block. This assumption is dead wrong. Between hanging with me, around some real older G's around my way and having two well–to-do parents, she's well gamed up on those fake sophisticated cats. And the horn dogs, well, they tend to know they're overly matched. If you come at her with any street slang and couldn't convey your thoughts with complete and concise sentences, she would eat you alive. This had its ups and downs, as far as I was concerned, because a lot of times she would make some of my friends feel like she was trying to be uppity, when in fact actually she was just being her facetious self. All of this and the fact that she was fine as California on a sunny day, was the reason she was my ace.

I'm just waking up good in the mid-morning, at about 10:30 A.M. The phone rings. I answered with my usual "Hella." On the other end the sweetest voice you ever want to hear replies, "Wake up William." It was Sabrina. I was like, "Don't call me William, my name is either Willie or Will or Willieworld. You know the rules, pick one." She replied, "Anyway. Your mother named you William, so I'll call you William." I snap back, "So you're my mother now?" She replies, "Yep. I'm your mammy, or at least that's what you call me when I'm putting it on you." I reply, "Anyway what's up with you girl?" She says, "I'm still getting all my classes situated and buying all my accessories I'm going to need for my dorm room." To this I ask her if she got the mirror too. And she replies, "Mirror, for what?" I answer, "Over the bed, silly. I have to see what I look like while I'm stroking." To that she starts laughing and says, "Shut up! You so crazy." To which I reply,

"That's why you love a nigga." And she says, "You know it. And you love me too nigga. Isn't that right?" And I reply, "You know you don't even have to ask. You know I love you girl."

After that exchange we have some small talk back and forth about what she's been up to and what I've been up to and catch up on current times. A lot of times after I do dirt I like to kick it with my girl as a way of cleansing my soul of my evil deeds. I mean,it's not like she's a saint or anything like that, but in my world she's about as close to divinity, as I'll ever get. I don't say this to imply that I'm some super thug who needs to see the light, but I'm saying this as a nigga who needs to clean up his act from time to time. When I dip into Sabrina's world, as I like to call it, I feel like I can be somebody. You see, her mom and her dad always treat me like I'm their son. And with their status, that means a lot to me. You see, Sabrina's mom is the Vice President at Bank of America and her dad was Chief Financial Officer at East Bay Mud, who everyone in the Bay Area knows as the people that keeps your water running. Thus, my affectionate knickname for her pops is "water boy". Her parents never really tried to sweat me about my future. They know I come from a blue-collar family and I was going to be the first from my family to go to college. All they ever did was encourage me to go to school and graduate. They always told me it was easy to go to college. The hard thing to do was to graduate. Believe me, I took all of their advice to heart. Sabrina loved the fact that her parents liked me. In her mind, I was not a square, nor a thug. She knew I was safe enough for her to introduce me to her parents and streetwise enough to satisfy her appetite on the wild side. Now, for me, this wasn't necessarily the greatest of things. If I strayed too far to either side it was all bad for me. There have been times when we've clashed for this very reason.

All in all, I knew she was the one for me, because she had too many intangibles that I liked. She was smart, beautiful, had attitude and most of all, she loved me. Our relationship was on cruise control status now because we knew each other so well, but she's proven time and again that she would do anything for me. This is why I have such a hard time within myself from time to time. I know I love my girl but, I just can't help myself from trying to hella at any breezy that I feel is attractive. It's like my dickhead is smarter than my bighead.

My moms tells me it's in the family blood and I can't say I disagree, because my grandpa was always in trouble with my grandma behind some skirt he was chasing. I just chalk it up to that and the company I choose to keep. All of my boys have multiple partners. From the most quiet ones like T-Bo, to the most flamboyant, D-Luv. I guess in my mind I have to make sense of this somehow.

Another thing that I think drives my behavior is the fact that each female represents a different side of me. Right now I was dealing with Anitra, Belize and Sabrina. My own little holy trinity. You see, Anitra brought out this feeling inside of me that let me be myself. By this I mean there was no being on point all the time like when I'm with Sabrina. Anitra was more of a plain Jane. She liked to spend time together whether it was creeping off to the movies or just staying at home chillin'. We could have a good time just sitting there talking about life. Not to sound conceited or anything like that, but I think that she got a kick out of talking to me because I seemed to have a little more intelligence than she, or at least that was the impression that both of us got. I would open her brain up to things that she never thought of. For instance, one time we were talking about good, evil, God, the devil and things like that, and I was telling her this story. It was about how the devil used to be the leader of God's choir in heaven. She didn't believe me until I started breaking it down. I told her that it was said that Saint Lucifer (the devil) was the most handsome angel in heaven. They also said that his voice was so beautiful that when he sang gold, diamonds, and rubies would come out of his mouth as he sang.

I told her I didn't know if this was meant literally or figuratively but that's how it was explained to me. It was also explained to me that this is why secular music sounds so much better than Gospel music. Well maybe not better, but more advanced, because the devil pretty much has control over the fleshly world. I told her that when Saint Lucifer got cast of heaven that he was so worshiped for his great looks and voice that one third of the angels chose to follow him to hell.

Things like this and stories about me and my potnas would blow her mind. In a way it was a stroke to my ego to have a girl just sit there, and look into my eyes with total fascination, hanging on my every word. I guess she satisfied my need to be worshipped, in a sick sense. I think all people need to satisfy that need from time to time.

Belize and I had a totally different type of relationship. It was strictly dickly. We didn't get into deep conversations about what was going on in the world. We didn't talk about our future being or anything like that. We both wanted to take the other one to their sexual limit. It was a relationship that T and Shea envied, because after that night we all kicked it together, their relationship with the breezys they chose were somewhat lukewarm. They would still kick it but the females would make them jump through hoops just to get a taste. On the other hand, if Belize called me, she wanted some wee-wee. If I called her, she wouldn't say no.

I loved it. My potnas really tripped when I told them that even when she was on her period, she would break me off some dome if I called her. This caused Shea to dub her "Queen dome". I would be lying if I told you we never had "any" type of conversation with one another, but it was mostly superficial. Through the superficial conversations, we began to learn quite a bit about one another, but really, how could I ever truly respect this girl who fucked me after I just boned her partner, without even washing my wee-wee beforehand? How could she truly respect me, knowing I'm bonin' her girl and I have a steady girl, too? It was really some sick shit but, hey, it works.

Last, but most certainly not least, there's Sabrina. Most people wonder how I could fix my lips to say I love this girl when I have my other two chicks so intertwined in my life. Well it's simple, I just do. Maybe it's too early for Sabrina and me. By this, I mean Sabrina is where I see myself ten years from now. She's got it all, but maybe I'm not ready for it all yet. Maybe I'm too immature to handle a young lady of her stature so soon, and that's why I supplement my ego with these other women, to make myself feel adequate. I can't say for sure but I think that holds some truth. I mean I find myself so deeply into her at times that I think I use these other woman just to balance my sanctity, so I don't catch myself falling too deeply in love and winding up getting hurt when she goes off to college. I can't say for sure, but if there were one that represented what I really thought I wanted in a wife, it would be Sabrina.

After everything is said and done, I find myself madly in love with one girl, liking to spend time talking with one girl, and loving the sex with the other. In Willieworld, everything is cool. At times I will look at myself in the mirror and ask the question, "What the fuck are you doing?" Then I'll answer to myself, "Living and having fun." And that'll be that. That has to be the answer that comes into my mind, because if I tried to make sense of my little world, I would go crazy. Things didn't really make any sense but I was happy. A lot of people envied my little kingdom I liked to call my world, so I knew I had to be doing something right. Something tells me someday I'll have to pay for all my joyful sins, but until then I'll have my three girls and a smile.

Me & T

Mr. Terrance Bronson was the jock of the clique. It was amazing to us that the biggest one in the clique was the one that never really wanted to play-fight, wrestle or roughhouse with any of us. I mean, even D-Luv would get in on the in from time to time. But T-Bo was always like, "Go on with that. I ain't tryin to hurt nobody today."

Then again, I remember the incident that probably put him in that state of mind for the rest of his life. One day T, Shea and I were chillin at Shea's watching 20/20 or something. D was out doing his thing, like he usually was for seventy percent of the time, and us three were just watching the idiot box, drinking and talking shit in general. There was something on about how blacks and whites were treated differently in America.

It was cool because it was stimulating our brain cells, which we were killing by drinking, but hey, it gave the brain cells we were killing one final thought before they exited the universe. In hindsight, I should've figured things could get out of control. I was sitting and watching a report on race relations, with Jackie Robinson and a fake Muslim that ate pork and boned white girls.

T and Shea were definitely bi-polar. T was open to pretty much everything. He dated females of all races. He kicked it with whoever was cool, no pre-conceptions. T would never surprise me with the cats he'd be with or bring around us; they were generally good people – no one I would ever spend a significant amount of time with, but good people nonetheless. Then again, you have Shea. He was the most judgmental person I had ever been around. He had an answer to every question, a remark for every comment, and a fake philosophy for everything about the white man. If he didn't eat bacon one day, it was swine; if he boned a white girl, he was doing it to show her how much disrespect she had for her by fucking a nigga who didn't give a fuck about her (supposedly); or if you said, it was a blue card (and it definitely was), he would say it was purple just because he didn't feel comfortable unless he was disagreeing with someone. Sounds sick, but it was true.

So we were watching this special and it's showing how white people can walk in department stores and shop freely and every time a black person would go inside the same store, they would be greeted by the same shopper every ten or fifteen feet with this cheesy smile and nod. Now as black men, we know what most white people think of us. So some of us (like me and T) would just figure it's just a small section of racist assholes that are so paranoid that the thought of a black person with money to spend is completely out of reality. As a result of this thinking, you kind of look at the problem that we were watching and think, "what else is in new?" Shea, on the other hand, wanted to make a big deal about this, as if he didn't ever receive this treatment himself and he was witnessing it for the first time. He was into this big triad, the white man this, and cracker that. T and I were looking at him like, "shut the fuck up". But the way Shea was wired, that look meant to him "oh, I'm getting on your nerves, let me dig a little deeper". Little did he know, this night he was digging a little too much for T's liking.

The program had moved on to their next story and it got silent for a second. I guess you could call this the calm before the storm. Then, as if to say, "you thought it was over, motherfucker", Shea starts in again on how white folks' evil mentality causes niggas to act evil in return, and he was jumping around with the hand movements and antsy behavior and out of nowhere T just says, "What up, Shea? You wanna wrestle?" Now I saw the look in T's eyes just before he asked Shea this question, and T looked like he was ready to break the wall on a kick-off. It was funny though, because right when he asked Shea that question, his whole facial expression changed as if it were a friendly proposition. Shea was not the village idiot (most of the time), but he was extremely stubborn. He knew he was getting on our nerves and he was probably about to feel the wrath – but stupid is as stupid does, so Shea answers, "Hell yeah, let's go the back yard so we could have room." Me, trying to play peacemaker, comes at them like, "Ya'll too drunk to be out here playing. Ya'll niggas need to sit down and just chill." But T was like, "Naw, this is gonna be the quickest slam dance you've ever seen." And Shea remarks, "Nigga please, size don't mean shit, compared to experience."

I'm just thinking to myself, I hope Shea has some type of health insurance. Shea opens the back door and a cool breeze comes in, special delivery from the Antarctic. Shea is like "Damn, it's too cold to go outside." T snaps back, "It ain't too cold nigga, come on out here and collect your whipping." Now Shea's attitude has swathed up a bit. You could see he was realizing that T was gonna bring it to him, but that's one thing I would always give Shea dap for. He knew T was about to manhandle him. To what extent, he didn't know, but all in all he knew he was in over his head and he still played it off until the end and went outside. Shea tried to rush T the first chance he got, but it was a very futile effort. Shea had his head down when he rushed in, so T just side-stepped him and grabbed his right arm and interlocked the two.

I was standing by, looking like I was watching an episode of *Cops*. Of course, doctor giggles got the best of me and I was laughing my ass off. To see the completely different looks in these niggas' faces was sheer comedy. You had the look on Shea's face which was "Oh my God, what the hell did I get myself into?" Then you had the look on T's face which was, "Yeah nigga, you know how long I've been waiting to do this." It was the thrill of victory and the agony of defeat, mixed with pleasure, pain and humility – a deadly cocktail for my boy Shea. With that said, T decided to finalize it. He pulled Shea back by both of his arms, twisted them up pretzel-style, gathered his weight, got underneath Shea and military-pressed him over his head. Before he did this Shea, was twisting out of control like a fish on a hook, but when T got him over his head he stayed stiff as a board. He didn't want to cause any balance that would make T drop him.

He tried to go to his cool voice and say, "Let me down, nigga stall me out." But T was relishing the moment. Not looking to struggling at all, he replied, "Say 'I quit, because I can't win'." Shea was like, "Hell naw," and T replied, "I got all night, boy," and Shea, being short on courage after being lifted in the air so easily, was like, "Fuck it, I quit because I can't win," and with that T let him down. I knew my boy T was strong on the football field but that was the first time I had seen him actually use that strength in another face besides football. It must've convinced Shea of something, because after that, he watched his behavior a little closer when it came to Mr. Terrance Bronson.

In the midst of all the excitement and kickin' it, we hardly realized the summer zooming by. It was almost time for T to be off to Cal State Long Beach on a football scholarship. We hadn't really dealt with the moments we were gonna have when T was here for the last time before he went away. I mean, we were together a lot but there was always an awkward moment right when we would say goodbye for the night. It always seemed like he would want to say something or I was stuck for words. At any rate, nothing was getting said.

One night, all that changed. The whole crew was chillin' one night at Shea's house. D was tired of dealing with the baller life for a minute and came to rest his mind from the street life. T was there by default, just fallin' through the spot after working out at the local nearby college. I came through on a whim — I had just come from Belize's crib, so I had stories to tell and didn't want to go straight home while the details were still fresh in my mind. And Shea — shit, it was his house, so he always blended into the scenery somehow. This night, I thought I was gonna steal the show with my explicit stories of how Belize was just turning me out at a ferocious pace, when my boy D-luv came with some ole serious shit. He finally told us about what happened with him and Cornelius.

T, Shea and I sat with our jaws wide open as he went into detail about the whole thing. How he, his cousin and another potna were getting at some chicks, some chicks left with his cousin and dude and left him alone, and Cornellius tried to check 'em. What he did in retaliation and everything. The look on everyone's face, to me, expressed "natural progression would've eventually led you to kill someone, but damn, you leaped stages quick." In our minds it was like a rookie quarterback taken in the first round, achieving success before everyone's prediction.

We were expecting to hear this one day, but damn. When he was expressing himself to us, he didn't really show any type of excitement. He didn't brag at all. It was almost like he was apologizing to us for following the path he took. We knew he liked the fast, glamorous life, but somehow we always hoped he would find his niche somewhere in there without having to be gangta-gangta. I think he hoped he would too. But now he was full-fledged. Once your name started ringing in the streets and you were a die hard person like D, it was only going to get louder and louder.

Now more things were starting to click in my head a little. For the better part of the summer, we (as in T, Shea and me) were getting a little more props then usual. We pretty much knew, associated or recognized everybody in the streets, but everyone took their position up a notch. People we really knew wanted to talk a little longer.

Associates' small-change conversation went up a couple of bucks and people we recognized said "what's up?", with a little more emphasis on recognizing us. All these people had something in common. They all heard through the grapevine, from someone whose information they really trusted, about D and Cornelius. According to everyone, they heard it from someone who was actually there when it happened. If that were the case the whole town would have been there. In any case, D told us it all.

We went into the back to play dominoes, drink and talk about the intricate details of our life and got to the point where everybody wanted to get out of the house and just ride. We wrapped everything up and hit the streets. D was driving, I was riding shotgun and T and Shea were riding in the back.

Our first stop was the liquor store, of course. We went into the local corner store, where the owner knew us from our numerous summertime visits. This man knew we were only eighteen and nineteen, but to him money was money. He knew we would only get someone else to buy it for us if he didn't sell it to us anyway, so pops (as we affectionately called him) would sell to us in the regular. It was so crazy when we went into the store this time. It seemed as though even pops caught the bug. Pops would usually just be like, "How you do'in?", with his best English impression. And we would just return in unison, "Ah-ight". He would just sell us our beer and tell us we needed to quit drinking. I guess that was his way of pleasing his conscience after selling beer to teens. But this time pops was like, "What up D?" And D replied, "Ah pops, you know me. I'm just hustling so I could own something like you." They exchanged a little more conversation as T, Shea and I slid to the freezer for the drink. When we got to the counter, pops and D were having a moment. D was laughing hilariously. He was like, "A-ya'll, look at pop's I.D." I guess D asked pops his name and D didn't believe what pops told him, so pops showed D his I.D. When we looked at the name on the I.D., it read, "Tom Xyouxiqong," and we were the next ones laughing up a storm. You see, pops was from Vietnam.

He came to the states five, maybe six years ago. We looked at his I.D. and figured when he came over, whoever sponsored him, told him the name "Tom" was the whitest, most American name a man can have — because that first and last name went together like "black president".

It just didn't look real, so pops showed us a little extra dap and shared more than a token moment with us and that was the first of many like experiences. When we were leaving the store, everybody was telling D how much of a fool he was for treating pops like that, and he was like, "That man tried to tell me his name was Tom, knowing damn well that's not what his momma named him." We laughed some more and piled into D's ride. We started riding, listening to some Spice One, as we drank and puffed on some of the dummy dust. We would always analyze every rhyme, cadence, word choice and production of every song.

This Spice One cat was off the hook. He had the tightest flow of any artist we had ever heard in the local area. The production went perfectly with his vocal arrangement. Instead of making the music and then letting him rap to it, it was like he did a rap *a cappella* and then tailor-fit the music to go with his rap. This added perfect background music to our smoking, drinking, talking to each other and stopping for the breezys.

Our ride would always start off with us choppin' it up heavy amongst each other through a various array of topics. It could consist of what was going on the streets: politics, movies, movie stars, singers, rappers, you name it. I always likened it to what philosophers did back in the day, except with us it was more like ghettosophy. We considered ourselves ghettospheres. We were all so set in our thinking that we always knew which angle the other would take on a given subject. This would go on a while until one of us spied a nice-looking female to pop at. The one usually spotting the eye candy first would be Shea. We would be riding and out of the blue hear, "Gat dammit, she looks good."

The conversation would stop and everyone would be at attention, everyone looking like a lion would look at a gazelle with a broken leg. Every woman was potential prey and it was a shame they knew it. I would always pull over and scope out the scene if one of us spotted one. Shea was the first to see one, as usual. D rolled up on her and checked out the particulars. She looked like she had been through the ringer a bit, so she wasn't up to D's caliber. She wasn't my or T's type, so it looked like Shea had one all to himself. When D drove up a little to give Shea his chance to talk to her, Shea looked a little jittery. He said, "Man, she don't look the same up close. Drive, man." We all looked at each and said, "Yeah right, nigga!" Shea could see from our reaction that she didn't look cool to us, and he didn't want to get clowned for getting her number, so he took the high road. What he didn't know is that we would never really have clowned him for any female he would get, because as far as we were concerned, he was a difficult ass. So honestly, we looked at it like "damn, he just missed out on some easy booty with big titties", but leave it to Shea. He's the most independent-thinking, letting-someone-else-change-his-mind person I know., so we shake that spot and start back on the streets to see what we could get into next. We were riding for about ten or fifteen minutes, just clowning Shea, when I spotted something real cool.

It was a little mini-flock of females. There was really only one problem with this. They were in a dipped out Acura with the fat rims and tight paint. Usually females like this would peek for a minute and then ride out. But this was unusual all around. The driver actually looked cool, and so did the other two females in the car. The fact that there were only three of them and four of us never entered into anyone's mind.

Well, anyone other than Shea, because we all knew who the odd man out was. There was an awkward moment every now and then, because it made Shea actually realize that he dwelled in Bizarre World and every now and then he got to kick it with the humans. But honestly, we weren't really expecting any action from these females anyway because they looked like high-saditfy window shoppers. However, when D pulled up next to the car and said "What's up?", the driver said, "Ain't your name D-Luv?" And D replied, "Who wants to know?" D and me was like, "Who are you? She replied, "Someone you would want to know."

So D was like, "Yeah that's me. And what's your name?" She replied, "Alexis". D told her she had a beautiful name and went into mack-daddy mode. He was polite and short with her. It was like he had his Mack game down to a science. No longer was there that long, "let me try to make her laugh to get in there good" conversation.

It was like his reputation preceded him. This bad chick that he was getting at just accepted what game he gave and was looking forward to his phone call. Neither T nor I ever got the chance to holler at the other two females, because D was so quick with it — but I don't think this was an altogether bad thing, because D said he was going to hook us up. D never lied about anything like this. The only bad part about it is it might take him a year to hook you up, but if he said he would, then he would. We continued on our expedition through the city streets.

This was actually the highlight of the ride to me. The time we would spend drinking, smoking, and riding the streets was usually the time when we would bond the most. We would learn a lot about each other through our conversations while we were riding. That's when D would open up and tell us about all of his war stories. T would tell us ambitions to be a Pro Football Player. Shea would too, about being a hater.

Just kidding. Shea would talk about things ranging from why people hated on him so much to why he would always keep a job, to keep from living on the streets when he was old. And I would talk about things like Utopia, heaven, hell, philosophy and ghetto paradise. I was the eternal optimist. It was cool; this particular night we had some good conversation and high times. The streets, on the other hand, were quite barren. We all got dropped off at Shea's and D drove off into the wind to get with his late night hype. Since T was about to leave, we decided to stay the night at Shea's to get in some last-minute bonding. T, Shea and I were really the three in our foursome that kept the glue together.

D was like an enhancer. We stayed up a while before Shea announced he was about to go upstairs and head into Bizarre World, otherwise known as sleep to him. T and I stayed up and had our long-awaited serious sit-down. We commenced with a little small talk and all of a sudden T said, "What do you mean?" And T said, "Exactly was I just said. What do you think of D?" And me being a little nane, is still not catching on. T was sensing this, so he just spelled it out for me. He said, "Look Willie, T loves all of you like brothers, but you know I feel a little closer to you then I do to D and Shea, and I think it's only fair if I tell you what I've been thinking. We both know what kind of nigga D is. We both love him but he made a choice to sell dope and kill. He is headed down a road I don't want you to get caught up in. And with me not being around, I'm not going to get the chance to be there and tell you when you need to chill on that nigga and when it's cool to kick it with him., so I feel as a good friend and as a brother I should tell you before I kept how I felt. I love you and I don't want to hear about shit happening to you."

I told T I knew what he meant and I would be careful. I had already been thinking the same thing in my mind, but I felt it would be worthwhile to express this to T. I told him, "I already thought about everything you said. I know D's name is hot and it's only going to get hotter, but the fact of the matter is, that's our potna, so if he wants to kick it and I'm down, then we're going to kick it."

T told me he understood but let me know I should be on my P's and Q's. He just let me know how much he wanted me to go to the local junior college, transfer and get my degree. And I reiterated how badly I wanted my season tickets to the Raider's game when he made their team.

We went on about how we hoped Shea would see the big picture in life and stop trippin' over the smaller things, and about some of our fun times over the years. Before we knew it, the sun was coming up and it was time to, finally, go to sleep.

Trouble at Shea's

Summer was still winding down. I was starting to look at the classes I would be taking at the local junior college, T was about ready to report at State College for his Football practice to start and D was steady ballin'; that left Shea. Shea's big brother would often joke about how his brother needed to get a job so he could help with the bills but now the jokes seemed to stop and the seriousness of the situation was starting to take over. The truth of the matter was Shea was out of high school and had no intentions of going to college. He was so far from a hustler it wasn't even worth considering, so what were his options?

A job? God forbid this suede-revolutionary working for the man. But Shea's brother wasn't playing. He was either going to get a job or work. D, T, and I were all curious at what Shea's choice was going to be and better yet, how he was going to spin it, so everything had worked out just as he planned. Before all this was going to take place there had to be the bitch and moan process. For a couple of weeks Shea would go on his little tirades about how his brother really didn't have a lot of bills to pay because they were living in the projects and the apartment was still in their mom's name. This was typical Shea. He didn't really trip off of the fact that his brother brought food in the house (which we all ate) his brother had a son of his own, his brother paid all utilities and things of that nature. I would think to myself at times, "Damn, if it wasn't for your brother, you wouldn't even be able to wipe your ass because you can't afford toilet paper. "But to Shea things like this didn't matter.

He would just twist it and say, "Well, don't he need to wipe his ass too?" if someone even thought of bringing it up. I would often sit and ponder how could someone who kicked it with such well-rounded people end up the way Shea was, but within my pondering came reason. Our crew was set up in a Darwinistic manner: the strongest moved up the ladder and weaker links slid down and took their position. On any given night, D, T andme ould fluctuate between one and three on this scale, depending on the breezy taste, but Shea would always be positioned number four. Well, he wouldn't always be positioned number four, but he was number four so often that if he was ever rated higher on the scale than any of us three, that person would be the butt of everyone's joke for a week or two, including the butt of Shea's jokes.

So hanging around with us would either breed thick skin or hetaerism. I guess Shea chose the latter. I think we stayed tight because within his hetaerism, he still had his cool points. He also knew the limits he could take his point of view with each and every one of us, because we hung around each other so much. Shea and his brother Jesse had a weird relationship. Jessie was a lot older and although he was cool, he also let it be known he wore the boxers in the house. For instance, one night, T, D, Shea and me were in the house chillin', there were a couple of extended hangers-on around on this particular night, and the house was off the hook. There were empty forty bottles everywhere, niggas was loved-talking and the scene was just outright savage. Usually, you'll find the owner of the house trying to keep the peace in situations like this, but not Shea. Shea was right in the middle of the loved-talking with everyone else.

All of a sudden the front door opened. It was like a scene out of a spaghetti western, with Clint Eastwood walking through saloon doors. It got quiet for a second when everyone saw Jess walk in. It got quiet for another second when everyone saw the expression on his face. Not to mention he had a pretty young female with him., but the expression on his face was that of a man who had been raped of his manhood. Not of a man who fought for his manhood and got it taken, but of a man who had been sweet talked out of his drawls and realized it when it was too late.

I have to give him credit though – Jess looked at Shea and said, "What's up boy? Let me holla at you upstairs." Shea was noticeably shaken but his pride made him stick his chest out like he was ready for battle. Shea bounced out of out of his chair and said, Ah-ight." The two of them went upstairs. Jessie's girl stayed downstairs. She had this look on her face of pure disgust. We were all sitting there like kids waiting for recess to began and hoping Shea would come back downstairs alive.

A few minutes went by and a couple of people started trickling out towards the back and front doors. Before you knew it, it was just D, T, Jessie's girl and me downstairs. When all of a sudden we heard, "Fuck you too, nigga!" It was Shea yelling at his brother Jess. Jess was like, "Get the fuck out then, nigga." Shea was like, "This is my momma's house and I ain't going nowhere!" Shea then turned his back on his brother and walked casually downstairs. The way he walked suggested, "Fuck you nigga. What the hell you gonna do about it?"

I know Jessie sensed this attitude from his younger brother because he followed him downstairs, throwing jabs with each step. Jessie was reeling them off, "That's why your ass can't get a job, that's why you're the laughing stock of your clique, that's why all your hoes look so ugly,"one after the other, like shots from a fully-loaded clip. No, make that a fully-loaded extended clip. It seemed as though this thing had been building up between these two for a long while and it just exploded.

You know Shea wasn't going to take this from his own. Shea snapped back, "You're just jealous." Jess was like, "Jealous? Jealous of what? Not having a job, being ugly, what?" Shea was like, "O.K. ugly. You know you wish you had half my hoes. That's why you got one here my age now." At this point things are getting interesting. T, D and me are just sitting on the couch mesmerized. All we needed was some popcorn and something to wash it down with. Shea and Jessie were snapping back and forth at each other like two wild pits. T tried to get up and keep the peace, but Jess looked at him and said, "Nigga, if you don't sit your black ass down, I'll jab you so many times, you'll be begging for a power punch." Shea barked back at Jessie, "Don't be talking shit to my potnas. That nigga ain't did shit to you. If you're gonna be mad at somebody take that shit out on me." Jessie replied, "That's what I thought I was doing, but if you feel like you want to take this to a higher level, we can."

When T, D, and me heard this, we all looked at each other, in slow motion like, "Oh No." We knew that Shea was not going to back down to this challenge. He looks at Jessie and says "Yeah, I want to make more of it, I want to take this shit to a higher level." And with that, "Boom," a quick jab to the chest. Jessie let off a solid close-range power punch to the chest of Shea. This blow was quick and powerful, but it was only a warning shot. It was hard enough to say, "Nigga I ain't playing."

But devoid of enough strength to suggest "Nigga, there's a lot more where that came from," Shea struggled to get to his feet. You know he was so embarrassed; he had to do something, anything to suggest "I ain't no punk "to these niggas. You see, Shea was too backwards that he didn't realize that we would gave him a pass if he had bowed down to his own flesh and blood. But man, Shea did give it the old college try. After he struggled to get to his feet, Shea let off a left jab of his own! "Pop." It too was quick and sharp, but it didn't come with the same velocity as Jessie's. Shea was looking for the same expression on Jess' face as he had on his own, when Jessie bombed on him. But instead, he got the look that a lion would give a hyaena after he just ate one of his cubs. This was another scene where T, D and I would reach for the popcorn, because this scene mesmerized us, like it was a pivotal part in a motion picture. Jessie's expression read, "Nigga, I know I can kill you, but you're my brother, so I'm only gonna mame you." He then grabbed Shea and shook the shit out of him. I mean it was like he was a 6'5" Robocop, shaking down a 5'2" punk, who just robbed a helpless old lady for her purse. It was just so brutal. Me, T and D were looking at each other, trying to see which one of us were going to break into laughter first. But instead we all snickered, and giggled, holding in each gasp of laughter so the two combatants wouldn't hear us.

This was all a moot point anyway, since the breezy Jess brought with him was peepin' the whole scene. Finally, D couldn't hold it in any further. "Ahhh!" D let out the loudest scream known to man. T and I were thankful. D gave us the perfect alibi to let off our own laughter. It must've been a scene of hysteria. Two brothers fighting on the steps nearby and one of the fighter's best friends laughing. On the sidelines, a breezy just came over to get some pipe, but instead got another crazy story to tell all of her home girls. From out of nowhere, the door opens. It was D's cousin Vell, who bounced in from time to time.

When it seemed like there were a lot of people around, he knew he was one of the few people who could just come and open the door without knocking. He saw the commotion and immediately tried to break Shea and Jess from one another. It was clear that he needed some help, but we were still in a state of hysteria, until Vell shouted: "What the hell ya'll looking at? Ya'll asses, up and help a nigga." With that, the mood changed instantly. We went from; all-out, carefree laughter to "Damn, now I gotta help this nigga." D helped his cousin with Jess and T and I subdued Shea. Jess was looking like, "Well I think I made my point. Now maybe this nigga will give me my respect." However, Shea looked like, "Fuck that! Now I'm a savage. If I'm gonna get my ass embarrassed like this, I'm gonna go all the way." T and I had to restrain Shea with all of our might. It was like Shea was maxing out all of the mighty strength we all knew he had within him. Jess, on the other hand, gave D and Vell this look like, "Nigga, if you don't get your hands off me…," and they simultaneously left him go. Jess then gave his girl this look like, "you ready to fuck?" At which time she gave him this look like, "Oh, I see you take pleasure in being a bully. I'm gonna give you the ass, but don't act like you didn't work for it in front of all of your friends."

But Shea had other plans. He didn't want to let this go. Jess could've really hurt Shea and Shea knew this, but he was so angered at being made to look like a kid in front of his friends that he snapped. We knew we were about to have a long night. Shea was looking at T and I like, "Seriously, let me go." T and I looked back at him like, "Look, we know you're upset with your brother, but nigga, recognize who you're talking to." At this time Shea, had no concept of this. He was worried about anything but his brother. He kept urging us to let him go.

He seemed as though he were calming down, so T and I gave each other, as well as Shea, the look. It was a look that suggested, "O.K., you're cool T, I'm cool, he cool,, so were gonna, let you go." Jessie wasn't paying any attention to Shea at this point in time. His whole mind had switched to pussy mode. He was smiling and joking with the breezy he brought to the house. Vell and D had adjourned to the back, probably handling street business. And T and I let Shea go. He walked off upstairs innocently. He went in his room and slammed the door. Jess and his girl looked at each other like, "Oh, the little boy was beat into submission." At this time, we all felt the same vibe but damn, were we all off the mark. Jess grabs his girl off the couch and says "Let's go upstairs. It's time for daddy to tap that ass. I think you've been a bad girl today." She comes along willingly like "Nigga, for me to be letting you talk all this shit, you better knock the bottom outta the safe and leave no change for the unfortunate, 'cause I'm horny and wet as hell." They both were looking for their moment of ecstasy. Just then you could hear Shea's door open.

We were hoping that he was going to the bathroom upstairs or maybe even coming downstairs just to get some verbal adrenaline off his chest. But neither was the case. Nothing could've prepared us for the next scene. Shea came down the stairs with a deuce-deuce in his right hand, hollerin'; "Now what's up?" I couldn't believe it. This man went and pulled the ultimate coward move. He couldn't stand the fact that his brother embarrassed the shit out of him so he goes and gets a damn gun. If you think I was shocked, you could just imagine the look on Jessie's face when he saw this. But you have to remember these two are brothers, so stubbornness must be part of their genetic makeup, because soon after the look of shock, Jessie's facial expression soon switched to, "Ah, hell, naw! I know this little nigga didn't just get a gun to kill me?"

I was still stuck on "Damn, I didn't know that nigga had a gun." Jessie pushed his hysterical date aside and said, "Nigga kill me. You got the heart to pull a gun on your own flesh and blood, then have the nuts to squeeze the trigger! Come on, nigga!"As much heart, nerve or audacity Shea had to go get the gun, he didn't have it to point it at his brother.

Shea had a look on his face I had never seen. It was a spaced-out look like, "What the hell am I doing?", mixed with, "You don pulled a gun, dumbass, what did you expect was gonna happen?" Shea knew he wasn't going to kill his brother and his brother knew Shea wouldn't kill him. But there is always that five-percent doubt, which is also the reason why Jessie didn't rush Shea and the reason why Shea wouldn't point the gun.

The devil is always working. If he could catch that five percent of you willing to go all the way at the right or wrong time, things could go from good, to bad, to worse in a matter of seconds. Jessie starts to yell at Shea, as the tears start to swell in his eyes, "Nigga, I love you and this is how you re-pay me? I pay all the bills, buy your clothes and let all your potnas kick it in this motherfucka and this is how you re-pay me?" Tears start to stream down Shea's cheeks as he emotionally replies, "I love you too, but you treat me like I'm shit. You're always makin' fun of a nigga."

"Talkin' bad about my hygiene, my potnas, my girls, and everything in between." Jess replies, "That's because I'm trying to light a fire under your ass, but maybe I'm doing it the wrong way. You got your potna D ballin' out of control on these streets, T is going to State on a football scholarship and Willie Wood, who's smarter than all ya'll and is going to the local junior college with a plan. And what the hell are you doing? You sit around here eating, shitting and farting, not worrying about the years to come. You got smart potnas man. You need to get up on game and start thinking about what you want to do with your life. I wanted to give Jess a standing ovation for his speech; for me, at that time in my life, that speech he gave put Malcolm X, and Dr. Martin Luther King Jr. to shame.

It was the most compassionate thing I ever heard in my life to date. With that, Shea said, "I love you, bra."And Jess said, "I love you too." They both took steps toward each other and shared a deep hug. During this hug, we noticed Jessie, while Shea was hugging him, and confiscated the gun from Shea, saying, "I'll take that." Shea relinquished the gun with no resistance. During the episode, the scene captured D, Vell, T and me. Everyone seemed to detach themselves from their isolated little worlds and joined in a moment of realness. Everyone kind of trickled out from there. D and Vell seemed as though their conversation in the back was the pre-plain for the late night activities, so they left together. T said he needed to get up early in the morning to go, and he left right after D and Vell. I really had nothing to do the next day and none of my breezys were paging me, so I hung around for a while. Jessie just looked at me and said, "Nigga, don't you have a home?" I looked back at him and said, "Yeah, nigga. Right here. He just looked at me and gave me this (snide) little chuckle, gave his chick the, "bring your ass on" motion, and off they went upstairs. Shea came down and sat on the loveseat to my left.

We watched a little television in silence, then Shea broke out with "My brother was right," in a somber voice. I was like, "Right about what?", as if I didn't share the same sentiment as him already. "He was right about me and you guys man," says Shea. I was like, "Man, you guys got a lot off your chest, and everything seems to be looking to be for the better."

Shea was like, "I know that, but everything he said was true. You, T and as demented as his world may be, D have your feet to the pavement. You guys are starting to make moves towards your destiny and I ain't thinking about shit but tomorrow." I interrupt Shea and say, "Max you're only eighteen years old. You're not supposed to know what you want to be when you grow up yet. Shit, I'm only going to college because it seems like the right thing to do. T is going to college because he has a football scholarship and shit, D is selling dope. What the hell future is in that?" Shea replies, "I know all of that man, but you guys are doing something – you have a start." I tell him, "It ain't too late for you, so don't even get to thinking like that. You could still register for school. You can get a part-time or full-time job, or do whatever you want to do."

"We're young nigga, the world is our oyster." At this time, I'm starting to sound like my mom and dad when they talk to me, so I try to cut the conversation before it sounds like I'm preaching, but Shea is looking like he's waiting for more, but I can't oblige him right now. I think what I said was enough, because he looked like he might have been enlightened a little. I can't say for sure, but I think this might have been the night that changed Shea's life. He was right in a lot of ways, when he explained to me that he really didn't have direction in his life, but being around people who did have things going on in their lives made him think.

He knew he couldn't just stay stagnant because D, T and I were trying to make moves. Shea felt inferior, although he wasn't, in my eyes. This in itself said something, because if Shea had no morals or even pride he wouldn't have felt bad that his friends were doing things and he sat on his ass all day. The fact he acknowledged that he wanted to find something he wanted to do (in his own weird little way) to feel like a productive person was a good start. All Shea had to do was try. Don't look at what everybody else is doing, just do for self.

And with the event that just happened with him and his brother, it made him realize a couple of things: his brother loved him and recognized he was about something and didn't want him to fall behind the curve, and that he had to take a look in the mirror. Deep down, Shea already knew everything he was told on this night. Sometimes you just need, broken down to you in the most carnal of forms for you to understand, things that are staring you in the face. And it gets no more carnal than brother against brother. Just ask Abel about Cain.

Critical Decisions

Now things were starting to look a lot different. I started my classes at the local junior college; Shea landed a job at Taco Bell. T was getting used to not being the big man on campus and D was a full-fledged D-Boy.

In its own way, things just sort of fell in place. Life was serving us little changes and we all adjusted accordingly. Now, instead of having almost nightly calls from T, I only got them from time to time. I would usually give him the ghetto CNN, on what's going down in the streets. I saw D a lot less but when we saw each other now, it was a lot less personal. D seemed to get a lot more into baller mode. We used to feel each other when we spoke but now I could see he was too much on the go to really stop and talk, and I was a lot busier with my studies.

Shea was pretty much the same, only Shea. Now he had his feet a lot more on solid ground, because he has a little money in his pockets and he was paying some bills. He remained that asshole who always had an opinion that was supposed to carry more weight than yours, because he had just enough responsibilities to say he was a responsible person but not enough responsibilities to know what the real world had in store for him.

School was just hitting full stride for me. I could get used this going to school at nine and being out by twelve routine. It was not too much different from high school as far as difficulty of subject matter, but you had to be a lot more disciplined, because you had no one on your back telling you when to go to class and there was no disciplinary action for not going to class, besides being dropped from the class. I was starting to meet new people, but I really wasn't interested in making too many new friends, so I would just say "hi" in passing and keep going about my way. You can't help but meet new people in an atmosphere like this though, because everyone was a lot more liberated and felt freer, without the constraints that high school provided. I was still seeing a lot of familiar faces I went to high school with, but I was also noticing some of the new female faces on campus. My girl was away at UCLA and I felt like a little peon in her world. We would still talk but I could see she was falling into the wrong hands. Our first conversations while she was at school was filled with "I miss you," "I miss you too," "I can't wait until vacation," and things like that. All of a sudden, she meets a couple of friends and now it's like, "I'll call you back when I get a chance," "so and so is here, let me call, you right back."

"Now, in my own little world, I'm a player and will continue to be so. So however much it pains me to see my heart (Sabrina) starting to spread her wings and start having more time for other people than she has for me, shit that's how I've always treated her. And no matter what the situation, fair exchange is not robbery, in my book.

My daily schedule was pretty much set in stone now. I would wake up in the morning, hit my push-ups and sit-ups, shower, go to school, be out of my last class by noon, study for two hours, go home and call a breezy (preferably Belize), set up my late night hype, chill at the house for a couple of hours and then head to Shea's to kick it. Life was good. My mom and dad said, as long as I stayed in school, I didn't have to work.

I was like "damn, I hope I can stay in school forever." I saw quickly though, that the consequence of this was being broke. I wasn't too much with that concept, so I always thought of different hustles that would put some change in my hands from time to time. One thing I quickly noticed was that everyone in college loved to get high but no one ever had access to weed on campus. I knew I had to quickly get in touch with D. I did that, "boom". Now I'm the man to see on campus. Initially, I overheard two females talking about getting high after their last classes, and I approached them with the best advertisement in the business, a free sample. I gave the ladies a fat suck and their mouths did the rest. I had no ambitions of being like D but I guess I provided the gangster element for us squares in school. Speaking of gangster element, D was in full stride. He was the man. Any time we went to a local club, D's name was ringing. When anyone fell in at Shea's, the first thing out of his or her mouth would be, "Damn, yo boy D is off the hook" or something of that nature. All the females were jocking him. D, his cousin Vell and their potna Nino, were like the street trinity. You would rarely see these cats separated now. Everyone knew Vell and Nino were stone-cold killers, but since D sent Cornelius to the afterlife, he too had the killer reputation. It was rumored that since then, he sent a few more people to join old Corny.

Personally, I preferred not to know the truth myself. All I knew was that all of the opposition had mysteriously disappeared, and it was better to be a friend than to be a foe. It was said that between the three of them, D, Vell and Nino had done just about every female in the town. And the truth of it was, if it wasn't totally true, it wasn't too far from the truth. Every time I saw any of these cats with females, their faces would be interchangeable.

There would definitely be different faces from day to day, and a lot of time from day to night. D always had a super bad chick with him but it was also said that he would have some rat heads on the late night. And honestly, they would only be considered rat heads in the daytime, because they were females with bodies that wouldn't quit but faces that had to quit. The kind of girls that cats would talk bad about in the day, with the general public on hand, but would give a call on the late night, under the cloak of darkness to do that dirty deed. I know all of this because a lot of the females he would be with on the late night would be the females I would tag from time to time or at least talked to on a time-to-time basis. I must admit though, some looked a little too bad for my taste. For instance, there was this one female named Kawana who looked like Shaka Zulu's lost twin, who D was later confirmed to have been sleeping with on the late night. I couldn't see myself even considering sleeping with this girl. She was tall, had nice-sized breasts and beautiful dark skin, but the compliments stop there. She also had no ass at all, nappier hair than a football player with an Afro who just took his helmet off in the fourth quarter, yellow cheesy teeth and hands that looked like she just peeled a thousand potatoes.

It truly baffled me, as to why my boy would stoop this low on the food chain, but I guess he really wanted to bone every chick in the town. Kawana was known to sleep with whoever, whenever, and a lot of dudes found themselves looking down at her face at one time or another, but I found the thought of that hideous, but hey, to each his own. So this was D's schedule, sex, money and hoes, not necessarily in that order.

Shea's days parallel mine in a lot of ways. He would wake up, hit his push-ups and sit-ups and shower, but then after that, our schedules changed drastically. While I was off on my way to hit the campus, Shea would be sliding into his brown Taco Shell uniform. When I first saw him in this, I couldn't help but laugh. He just took to it so naturally. When we were in high school and would go out we would laugh at all the fast food workers who we used to go to school with, never thinking we would find ourselves or any of the homies there.

Shea would come out of his house and the sun would beam on his pants and give them this certain little gleam. It was as if his pants were talking to the public at large saying, "I'm not just some normal pair of brown pants, look at my sheen. I work at Taco Shell nigga!" Maybe it was the mixture of oil, taco sauce, sour cream, and washing detergent. No other pants you could buy in the store would look like the pants fast-food workers wore. Shea made a valiant effort to try and make his uniform look a little B-boyish by getting his a bigger size than they needed to be and by tilting his hat to the side, trying to look like big ole player but we knew it was Shea, so he couldn't sell anyone on that dream. Although I must admit, I'm proud of my boy. A lot people wrote Shea off before he ever got started. The consensus was that he would never have a job and he was going to be another victim to the streets. However, I think the argument Shea had with his brother Jess lit a fuse in my boy. I heard he was actually one of the better employees at the Shell. He was never late to work, he was a fast learner and he even went the extra mile, holding his attitude in check when dealing with disgruntled customers. Shea paid his brother on time, all of the time with his little bills and managed to keep a little extra change in his pockets.

I found myself in Shea's world more often these days, since D and T aren't around, Shea and I started spending a lot more quality time together and believe it or not, it wasn't half bad. T's world was a lot different these days. Gone were the days of "Oh, T, you scored six touchdowns, can I suck your dick?" It was now like, "Yo, fresh meat, get me some water, bitch." T didn't like this at all but he knew it was part of the routine.

Everybody had to pay dues, that's what I love about every nigga in my crew. We all knew you had to pay dues. I had to take my ass to junior college, Shea had to wear the brown bagger, T had to fetch water and D had to kill. However bad or good this may seem to a person, we all paid our dues. T would call me in the best of moods, glad that he was able to get away from home and all of the negativity. We would constantly find our way around, and he would call me crying sometimes because he missed home.

The boy had never been out of a fifty-mile radius from where we grew up in his life for more than five hours, which was the time it would take to drive to a road game, play, and drive home. He would talk about coming home and leaving school because things were too hard, and I would talk to him like the bitch he was being. We would have a few laughs and he would be back to dealing with his situation. Things weren't easy for any of us, but they could be a lot worse. For instance, we have this potna named Tory, who was just doing bad. It didn't really come as a shock to any of us that he was going down the wrong road. The surprise was how fast he was looking bad. We had just graduated high school and my boy was looking like he hadn't had sleep in ten years. He would hang in front of the local mom and pops store asking for change and we would be like, "Nigga, moms only gave me twenty for myself, how in the hell am I supposed to break you off when I can't even support myself." This really tripped us out. I couldn't get used to the concept of standing in front of a liquor store and asking friends and strangers for change to buy alcohol, weed, or whatever vices a person might have.

But like I said, no one was surprised to see Tory doing bad. His mom was an alcoholic who slept around with so many niggas, Tory didn't even know who his real pops was. The one sucker, oops, I mean dude who stepped up to the responsibility of taking care of Tory was so upset that his moms slept around, he looked at Tory as a symbol of this, so he would treat him like shit all of the time. This always bothered Tory and it was no surprise why he took the easy out. On top of all of this, when crack hit the projects both his moms and pops took to it like flies to shit. I felt sorry for Tory but I really couldn't feel too much sympathy.

True enough, his parents were fucked up, but sometimes you have to be that strong person to break the cycle. It's easy for me to say, seeing as how I have moms and pops who taught me right from wrong, but this nigga had enough positive influences in his surroundings to have chosen a better route for himself. So, all in all, I would have to say that my boys and I weren't doing too badly. The one I really worried about was D-Luv – sure he had the most material things out of all of us at this time but I really thought he could be doing so much better. D was an intelligent cat and if he felt college was an option, I know he could breeze right through it. But with each day that went by I knew there was less chance of that happening. In fact, for me to even think that it could happen in the first place was very naïve. I mean this dude was making thousands of dollars per week without putting in much time or effort, and he was drilling any and every female he wanted. Now let me see, school where you had to study, be broke, and manage your studies or hustle, where you made your own hours, made cash, and had any girl you wanted. Those weren't very difficult choices. I just pray every night that my boy is not the next one I read about in the local section of the Oakland Tribune getting raided by the cops or even worse, being shot and killed.

The Trip

Life was still moving along and taking its course. For me, the course was really starting to look bad. moms and pops would always have their ups and downs in their relationship, but after twenty years of marriage they were calling it quits. I really couldn't believe this shit.

I mean, how could you be with someone for twenty years and just decide one day that you're too different to get along anymore? This situation threw me for a loop. I wasn't like the average kid who just blindly sided with moms when things like this happen. I loved both of my parents so much I didn't know what to think. The good thing about it was, there was no dirt slinging. Whatever was really at the core of them going their separate ways stayed between the two of them. My mom had nothing but superlatives for my dad and my dad likewise for my moms.

This made it a little more confusing for me, though. I wondered why they had all of these nice things to say about each other if they wanted to be apart so bad. I wouldn't wonder too long, though. I guess my parents agreed that my dad should sit down and explain exactly what was going on so I wouldn't be left with too many questions. My moms told me she had to go and take care of some business and pops called me into the living room. As I walked in, I noticed a fifth of Christian Brothers Brandy on the table along with two shot glasses.

The lights were dim and pops was sunk deep into the leather sofa. He looked at me and said, "Son it's time we had a man-to-man talk." I've seen my pops look serious before, but he had a different look this time. Usually when we would talk seriously it was more like he was talking at me. This time he seemed to be talking to me with a warm seriousness.

He bent over, twisted the cap off of the brandy and poured two shots. He said, "Son, I want you to have a drink with me and listen. Just listen." I then bent over, grabbed my glass and took a sip, like the accomplished drinker I was. Pops just looked at me and gave a little smirk as if to say, "Oh, you've been at this a while haven't you boy?" Pops then grabbed his drink and began to speak. He said, "Son, let me preface this by saying, I love you and your moms with all of my heart, but sometimes things just happen in life. Your mom and I have had problems throughout our relationship, but we always chose to keep them behind closed doors.

"We agreed that you need her love and warmth as well as my strength and discipline in the same household at all times., so no matter what problems we had between us we agreed to stay together until you came of age." At this time I start hitting my brandy again because I'm thinking, "Damn, the only reason my parents stayed together was because of me. Were all the smiles fake? Were all of the happy times fake? I mean was my life fake?" This shit had me bugged. But my pops, being the cool cat he was, broke it down for me. He went on, "Willie, don't think you were the only reason your mom and I were together. We really did and still do love each other, but it's a different type of love that I hope you never come to know." I interrupt my pops and ask, "If you guys still love each other, there has to be some way you could work out whatever is going on wrong, right?" Pops, seeing the desperation in my eyes, answers bluntly, "NO, Willie! Our love is very much on a friendship level now. There are no details you're going to hear about that will give you the reason your moms and I decided to go our separate ways, but there was no cheating.

"We didn't decide to get married because your mom was pregnant with you or anything like that. We are just two strong individuals who decided to call it quits. We both love you and what's going to be done is just what's going to be done." And that was it. Pops was always short and to the point throughout my life and in his exit from the house, he was the same. We continued to polish off the Christian Brothers and talk about less important things pertaining to the big picture, but things that made the situation easier. As the bottle got lower and lower, we began to open up more and more. Pops kept re-iterating how I had to be the man of the household and look after moms in his absence and let me know he was going to be in an apartment fifteen minutes away, and if I needed to talk he was only seven digits away. I left our conversation with a little more comfort in my heart but nothing can really ease the pain of your parents getting divorced but time.

Now as if I wasn't receiving a low enough blow with my parents going through it, I'm starting to hear a little buzzing going around, about Sabrina fucking around with the star running back at UCLA. It being rumored by some people we went to high school with that were a couple of degrees separated from my inner circle, so I couldn't really put too much stock into it. However when my boy T told me, it was all but confirmed in the college circuit. I had to deal with it.

I would call Sabrina and try to confront her with these accusations, but she wouldn't do anything but deny it. I must admit I trained this girl very well in the art of denial, because if she cornered me on something and even if her best friend saw me with her own eyes doing something, I would deny it to the end. But she was still a rookie, so she would make major mistakes like telling me I couldn't come to see her for a weekend because she was going to see the football team play on the road with her friends when I would be watching their home games on television. This was a major mistake on her behalf. However, I never confronted her with this. I had a better plan. My boy T had a game against UCLA. in two weeks, and you better believe Shea and I had a road trip coming up. I know I was at home doing my thing but fuck it, Sabrina was still my ace and I had to see what the hell was going on with my own two eyes.

Time seemed to be creeping by for the next twelve or thirteen days. With each day that passed another piece of the thousand-parts puzzle would gradually fall into place. I saw D and he asked what I had been up to and I told him not much, but T had a game versus UCLA and Shea and I were going to make the trip out there. And just like clockwork he says, "Oh you gonna check Sabrina while you're out there?" And I'm like, "What makes you ask that?" He says, "Come on man, you know I'm the word on the street, and word on the streets says she's fuckin' the star running back down there."

I reply, "Nigga, you heard this and you didn't holla at your boy?" He replied, "Ay man, I just figured you knew or had an idea about it. And you know I ain't the type of nigga who likes to gossip. I know you're a playa and you can handle yours, so I kept it to myself. Besides, if you was a square and wasn't doing a gang of fucking yourself that would be the only way I would've even pondered putting that in your ear."

So I asked him, "Why did you say something now?" His response was typical D and he hit the nail on the head. He said, "Well I know you love our boy T and all, but nigga I also know you heard the buzz on the street and you had to go see for yourself. You know — to get that closure people are always talking about." I then asked him why he used the word closure. And he replied, "Do you think all of the rumors aren't true?"

"I mean let's just break it down. A senior running back about to go to the league, who has boned every chick on campus, meets fine ass eighteen-year-old freshman with a body that won't quit and is smart as hell. Oh, let's add in the fact that she's away from home for the first time in her life, partying like it is going out of style and she hasn't got you there to serve her wee-wee when she's nice and hot." That is exactly why I loved D. He would break things down to the very last compound. I just looked at him, laughed and said, "You black mothafucker." We both broke out into laughter after this. I must say this put me in a whole new state of mind as to what I should expect when we reach that point in time. I honestly wasn't expecting to see Sabrina with this cat, but after talking to D, I realized if I wasn't expecting to see Sabrina with this cat, I was really dreaming. Another day passed and T gave me a call to make sure Shea and I were coming and to finalize our sleeping arrangements. T and the rest of his team were going to be staying in the Marriott, not too far from the campus and Shea and I managed to get a room in the hotel too.

We planned on kickin' it in my and Shea's room until T had curfew. We talked a little about what was going on in the town and how he was excited to be getting his first start in a nationally televised game. I was excited for my boy too. He had played linebacker and running back in high school and now seemed to be eager to run the rock and do big things. But all the conversations would lead right back to Sabrina. T was in the small minority that didn't believe Sabrina would get with dude. He told me this cat had a reputation for doing so many women that even when he didn't get the one he was aiming for, it was just assumed that he tagged her and didn't tell anybody. And since he showed interest in Sabrina, everyone on campus might have assumed that he did her already. T was always one to try and look on the bright side of things, but I felt my boy was way off base on this one. I told him Shea and I would be arriving early Friday evening. We were going to rent a car and drive down, so it would take us about six and a half to seven hours to get there. Shea was taking that day off work and I got out of class at twelve, so we would be leaving at about one o'clock. With that, T told he would see us when we got there and we hung up.

Time began to speed up as Friday came closer and before you knew it, I was in my last class Friday afternoon. I spoke with Sabrina on and off the last couple of days before. I planned the trip. She didn't have a clue that I was coming down there, but she could feel something was in the air. For the first time in a long while she was calling me, and we were having actual conversations. For the longest it seemed as though her goal was to get off of the phone as soon as I would call. Now, all of a sudden she wants to tell me how studies are going, why she can't stand this professor, how her roommate gets on her nerves and it was like we were actually loving friends again. Her sincerity almost lead me to believe I wouldn't catch her in the arms of another guy,, but I didn't want to get my hopes up too high.

I told her I had to help my pops move some of his things this weekend, otherwise I would probably try to see her this weekend. After I told her this she said, "Oh, I wish you could come down here this weekend because I need to feel your touch, but I understand you have to help your dad, so maybe sometime soon." In my mind, I'm thinking, "Sooner than you think." But I just replied, "Yeah, I'll see you soon." We then exchanged I love you's and closed our conversation

Thursday night. Now my last class is over. It seemed like it took hours for me to walk home from school, but it actually only took me the usual twenty minutes. I got to the house, peeled off my clothes and hopped into the shower. By the time I dried off and started to put lotion on, Shea rang the doorbell. I was like "Damn, only this nigga." I swear Shea is the most punctual nigga you ever want to meet and that's punctual to a fault. I yell downstairs, "Hold on! I'm still putting my drawls on nigga!" I heard back, "That shouldn't take you long, after all, to cover a wee-wee that small shouldn't be a hard task at all!" I yell down the stairs again, "Fuck you!" And I hear laughing outside the door. I put my pants and a wife beater on, and I go downstairs to get the door. "What's up with you and punctuality, nigga?" I say to Shea. He just gives me the head nod as if to say, "What up" back. He goes to the couch, and turns on the television and I head back upstairs. Shea yells out, "I hope you're packed, nigga! I don't feel like driving all into the night." I reply, "I'm already packed, and it wouldn't matter if I wasn't anyway because it's going to take us six and a half hours to drive there anyway. If I did have to pack thirty minutes wouldn't make much of a difference." There was silence for about one minute, and then I heard, "Hurry up anyway nigga." I yelled back, "Took you a while to do the math huh, Igor?" I let out a big laugh and continued to get dressed.

As I was throwing on some smell good, getting ready to carry my bags downstairs, I heard the door open and Shea saying, "Hello Mrs. Woodson." I heard my mom reply, "Hello Shea. How's everything going?" Shea replied, "Fine. Just working, paying bills." My moms replied, "Ooh boy, you're way too young to be talking like that, you got a whole lifetime ahead of you. You better have some fun before you get those gray hairs."

They shared a laugh and then moms came upstairs. "What up moms?" I say to her as she hits the top stair. "'What up?' What's up with you talking to me like I'm one of your little homeboys off the street?" "Moms you know what I mean," I reply. She says, "Boy, I know. I'm just playing with you. So you're leaving me for the weekend huh?" I replied, "Yes mom, you remembered I'm going to see Terrance play this time." My mom replies, "Of course I remember. I just want to give my baby a hard time before he leaves me. It's actually a good thing because momma is gonna party." I reply, "Party?" My mom says, "Yes, party. You gotta problem with that?" I say, "I guess." My moms says, "Damn boy, I was just kidding. You know, how you like to do to me sometimes. Don't have a heart attack. I swear sometimes you remind me so much of your daddy." I begin to make my way down the stairs and I could see the expression on Shea's face. Clearly, he's been ear hustling. I just shake my head and say, "Shut the hell up and let's go." Shea yells, "Good bye Mrs. Woodson." My moms replies back, "Good bye Shea, you and my son be careful out there." Shea and I reply at the same time, "We will!" And with that, we're out the door.

I brought two nice-sized bags along for the trip. Shea helped me carry one to the car. He was struggling mightily with the bag I asked him to help me carry. Of course it was the heavier of the two. Shea yelled "Damn nigga, did you decide to bring another date in your bag, in case you saw Sabrina hugged up with dude?" I replied, "Hey boy, that's hittin' below the belt. Unless you want to hear a million caps about how your face could be pressed into gorilla cookies, I suggest you slow down on the Sabrina jokes." Shea replies, "Oh I smell a little sensitivity in the air. Did you just fart or is that your cologne?" I had to laugh. Even though Shea would tell a million duds for jokes, he would get off a couple of funny jokes every blue moon. I knew the tone he told the jokes in weren't meant to be totally degrading, so I didn't actually feel too bad.

As a matter of fact, it actually lightened the mood. With that, we were in the car and I was off to look destiny dead in her eyes. We got on the freeway at about 1:30. There was absolutely no traffic, so it was smooth sailing down Interstate 580. Shea and I talked a little but listening and rewinding NWA, Ice Cube, Spice One and Ghetto Boys tapes really consumed us. We would always try to decide exactly what we thought each rapper was thinking when they wrote their lyrics. It was a trip. We were like ghetto philosophy dissectors. I would be like, "Cube meant this when he wrote that lyric." And Shea would be like, "Naw he meant this." We went back and forth between the NWA and Cube lyrics because they were funkin' something Terryble back in those days. What we really like listening to was Spice One.

This dude's cadence on his lyrics when he rapped just put him light years ahead of every other rapper out to us. The way he stuttered stepped and doubled up on words when he was bustin' was just so tight it was ridiculous. Well, all of this talking about music made us both thirsty. We stopped in Bakersfield to get us something to drink. We walked into the gas station slash convenient store. We immediately noticed there were no forty's and no Old English. We were like "Damn, what the hell we gonna sip on?" Begrudgingly, we decided to get a twelve pack of Budweiser. This was hardly our beer of choice, but any beer would be welcome at this point. I dug into my pocket to get some money and I pulled out the money my moms gave me for the trip. To my surprise there were three crisp one hundred dollar bills. I started to tally all of the money I had on me in my head. I was like, "hmmm… two hundred from pops, three hundred from moms, and three hundred seventy five from hustling my bomb. I almost had nine hundred dollars for the weekend and we already had the room booked and paid for and the rent-a-car was paid for through Sunday. The only expense I had for the weekend was food.

I was shining like fresh quarters for the weekend. To top all of this off, just as I'm pulling my money out and offering to pay for the beer and our little snacks, Shea puts some stuff on the counter and says, "I got it." I had to think to myself, "Hey, this weekend could still turn out to be good yet. What if Sabrina really missed me and me coming down and surprising her was going to be a good thing for the both of us?" This was highly unlikely, but anything is possible. After Shea paid for everything and filled up on gas, we got back on the road. The past two hours of our trip flew by. We drank, listened to some music and talked our way to Los Angeles. We got good directions to the hotel before we left and had no problems finding it. We rolled in the parking lot at about eight o'clock.

We got out of the car and both let out a big stretch after being confined in the vehicle so long. I got a chance to stretch a little bit, seeing as how I rode shotgun all the way here, but Shea really had to stretch because he drove all the way. We proceeded to get our bags out of the trunk and make our way to the receptionist desk. I gave the woman at the desk my name and she replied, "Double occupancy?" And I said, "Yes ma'am. I wouldn't want to be hugged up with this beast in the bed. Would you?" She looked at me like I was crazy and she handed me the key to the room.

Shea and I joked about the evil face the woman gave me and we took the elevator to the room. We were in room 315. As soon as we get to the door to go in the room the phone starts ringing. I fumble around with the keys, trying to open the door so we could answer the phone the only person we thought it could be was T-Bo. So, I finally get the door open and Shea rushes past me and answers the phone. He picks up the receiver and says, "What up nigga?" Right after that he just bust out into this hysterical laughter and says, "Yeah, we're in room three fifteen," and he hangs up the phone. I was like, "Who was that, T?" Shea was like, "Naw, it was your momma." I then said," Fuck you," and we both began to go through our bags.

Within the next five minutes, we heard a knock at the door. After a few more quick knocks the door began to slowly open. A big head creeps in through the door. It was none other than our boy T. "What up niggas!" T says loudly as he slides his way into the room. I say, "What up nigga!" And Shea says the same. We all run toward each other like some seventh-grade females that haven't seen each other all summer, on the first day of school. T says, "Man, I'm glad to see ya'll. I'm nervous as hell about starting tomorrow and since a nigga is a freshman I can't get too much love from my teammates. I needed ya'll bad for this one and ya'll came through like champs for me. Man, I appreciate this shit a lot."

"Yeah, Yeah," I reply. "You know daddy had to come and make sure his son did well in his first big game." Then Shea chimes in, "Yeah, since we really don't' know who the biological is, we both thought we'd come and see our son perform." T and I look at each other and T says, "Damn, who's been teaching this nigga jokes? He actually sounds like he has a thought process now. Could it be this nigga is actually making strides up the evolutionary chain?" Of course Shea has something antagonistic to say about this. He says, "Nigga you go to school for free. You play a game you love everyday. What the hell is so hard about that?"

T shoots back, "School isn't really the hard part, nigga, and as much as I love football, living this shit twenty-four seven takes its toll on you. I wake up at five in the morning, go down to the track and run a mile. Then, we get together in our position groups and go into conditioning drills. That shit lasts for an hour and a half then we go to the cafeteria to eat breakfast. We usually wind up kickin' it there for about an hour or so. Then it's to the dorms to shower up and be to class by eight o'clock. You can't tell me that you could do that shit everyday without it wearing on your body and mind." I then said, "Well the shit definitely shows. You're as big as a house and you look like you are even sleeker than you were before. I can't say much as to how it's affecting your brain, but if I was a rump ranger, I might have to holla." T laughs at my statement and then says, "I'm serious man. If I wasn't getting my chance to start tomorrow, I don't know if I'd be able to take this shit." I then say, "But you are and all that other shit is hindsight, so tomorrow when you get out there, take all that shit you got inside of you on the field and make it happen. You's a soldier at this shit man. You ain't no philosopher!" T and Shea both reply, "Fo' Sho!" Shea then starts to tell us some of his Taco Shell stories. I knew he was gaining a sense of self by having some money in his pockets, but I never knew how seriously he took his job until our conversation at the hotel.

Shea started telling us how he worked with the village idiots and how he was moving up in status so quickly there. The first thing that popped into my head was, "Damn, there are people who you actually think are village idiots, and secondly you're actually bragging about your status at Taco Shell." Shit, don't get me wrong, this is still my boy and I love him, but expectations have to be fairly low to be bragging to two college students about moving up the ladder at Taco Shell, but fuck it. To each his own.

At any rate, Shea tells us how his supervisor, in addition to having him counting the registers when employers start their day, also has him in charge of ordering all the lettuce, sauces and tortillas and stuff like that. I tried my hardest to hold back my laughter and succeeded. However, T didn't. He said, "Nigga, you done moved from the register to sauce duty, what the hell kind of progress is that? Holla at me when you're running that shit. Then I'll give you some dap for choosing that over school." Shea was like, "Don't worry. I'll have my own store within two to three years and then we'll see what's up." I looked at Shea and said, "You're serious? That's your goal for the next two to three years?"

Shea said, "As matter of fact, Yep." T and I just looked at each other and I said, "Shit, if that's what you want and you're happy, let it be done." We talked some more about how things were changing in our lives and then as if he dropped a nuclear bomb T says, "So what's up with Sabrina?"

Shea then turns to me and says "Yeah, what's up with my girl Sabrina?" in a most cynical way. I looked at them both and said, "Man I honestly don't know. I hope in the deepest part of my heart I don't catch her with this dude but I know I'd be a fool not to expect to see her with this cat. Either way it goes, it's all a part of the game that I'd chosen to play. Had I not been worrying about all the other pussy I was chasing and concentrating more on my relationship with Sabrina, we wouldn't be sitting here now talking about this shit." That was that. They both looked at me as if to say, "Damn, since you put it that way, I guess that is the procedure."

We went on talking until T had to go back to his room because of curfew. We told him we would look for him during warm-ups and holla at him after the game. He said, "Cool," and with that, T was out. Shea and I talked for a little while and we went to sleep soon thereafter. We were exhausted from the drive, so we had no problem getting to sleep.

My initial thoughts when I closed my eyes were on this light-skinned angel floating towards me, with this bright light behind her, beautiful, luscious spread wings and a golden halo over her head. It was none other than Sabrina. She approached me with open arms, with her hair flowing, and bare-naked skin. She was the most beautiful sight I had ever bore witness to. I look at myself and I was also naked. One thing that was awkward about this dream was I had no wings. I was a mere mortal in the presence of an angel and this was how I felt often in Sabrina's presence. Her angelic figure came closer to my mortal body and she gave me the warmest hug ever imaginable; there was no sexual presence felt.

I then hugged her back as passionate as I could, and then, Boom! The alarm clock goes off. "Time to wake that ass up!", says Shea in the most annoying-ass voice ever heard to man. "Turn off the alarm and shut the hell up," I say as I roll over to get up. Shea then says, "Damn you sure was doing a lot of mumbling in your sleep. What the hell kind of dream were you having nigga?" "Don't trip," I say as I begrudgingly slide out of bed to take my initial piss of the day. I then go ahead and get into the shower first since I was the faster thinker of us two. Shea's earlier comment to me soon came up and bit him in the ass, as he had the same look on his face when he got up to hop in the shower as I had.

T calls the room and gives me last-minute details about where we should be, what to look out for and things like that. Shea and I then start to make our trek towards the stadium. We have no trouble driving from the hotel to the stadium. The game started at one and the parking lot was full at eleven. We park and then find our way to the visitor section. All the while we're walking, my head is on a swivel looking to see if I could spot Sabrina anywhere. I did not see her but I noticed a lot of other beautiful women along the way. Just like a nigga. No matter what the situation, we're always looking for the better deal. Shea and I would look at each other every time either time one of us saw someone we thought looked cool. We caught ourselves looking at each other a lot during our quest to find the visitor section. Shea brought along a pair of binoculars to watch the game and I asked him why he did that, since we were in the front row. He replied by saying he wanted to look like a real fan. I told him, "What you're going to look like is a nigga with binoculars in the front row." We laughed and got our seats.

We saw T warming-up with the running backs, looking like a true stud. He spotted us and gave us the thumbs up. We acknowledged with head nods and finger pointing and we settled in. Time went by and it was time for kick-off. UCLA came out to blistering cheers and Shea and I looked at each other like, "Damn, our boy is in the big leagues." State college gets the ball first and T makes his big debut.

The first couple of series were three and out for both teams. Then there it goes, the big all-world running back for UCLA. He goes for an eighty-yard run. This dude looked like bison running free on the wild terrain. Again, Shea and I looked at each other. This time the look was like, "Uh, ohh, our boy is in trouble." After the kick-off T, gets the call on first down. Our boy got stood up by a linebacker and stripped by a corner back. The little dude stripped it and took the ball in for a touchdown.

Just then, Shea tapped me on the shoulder, handed me the binoculars and said, "Look." He pointed towards the UCLA side, around the forty-yard line. I looked and saw none other than Sabrina jumping up and down in her baby blue UCLA sweatshirt, screaming for her school.

After that sighting, I gave Shea back his binoculars and tried to give it no thought. He just gave me this look like, *The moment of truth is among us, son.* I looked back at him as if to say, "Fuck her, I'm a motherfuckin' player nigga!" It was a feeble attempt to be cool and I could tell because Shea then returned with a look as if to say, "Yeah, right nigga." The game progresses on and at the half, UCLA. is up 21-10. T was doing alright.

He had picked up a respectable forty yards rushing in the first half. The one big blemish was his fumble but he had another half to make up for it. At half time, Shea asked if I wanted to go on the other side and surprise Sabrina. I was like "No. I'm gonna wait it out until the end of the game and see what's up." Shea was like, "Alright." We went to the bathroom, got a couple of hot dogs and something to drink, and then returned to our seats. The second half was about to start. UCLA got the ball first and marched down the field like an army.

Their drive stalled at the end and they had to kick a field goal. The score was now 21-13. Before state was about to take the field again, our boy T looked at us with a sarcastic smile, as if to say, "Watch this." And watch we did. I don't know what lit the fire under T's ass but he looked like a totally different runner in the second half. In the first half, T looked like he belonged, but on certain plays he would look timid.

The second half was a totally different story. The first time he touched the ball in the second half was on a half back screen. T followed his blockers and they sprinted all the way for the score. T took a five-yard screen and turned it into a 73-yard touchdown. The score now was 24-20. After this score the momentum of the game seemed to switch. UCLA now seemed to go three and out every series. State was now getting yards in chunks. My boy T was hitting up for ten and twenty yards runs left and right. In between plays, I would give Sabrina a peek and she looked a little nervous now that State had the momentum.

State was only able to manage another field goal until late in the fourth quarter, even though they were dominating statistically. The score was now 24-23, with two minutes left in the game. State had the ball on their own twenty, and all three of their timeouts. On the first play they gave the ball to T on a draw. T took the ball and rambled off fifteen yards.

State let the clock roll; they handed off to T again, for another fifteen yards. Now at midfield and with a minute and a half left in the game, UCLA burns their last time out. UCLA taking a timeout at this point indicated that they thought State could possibly score a touchdown. At this point, T has over one hundred yards receiving and one hundred fifty yards rushing. Our boy went prime time on national television and stole the show. Now State goes back to work. They hand the ball off to T again. He rambles off ten more yards.

The clock is still winding and State is at the forty. Again they hand it to T and he sprints frantically towards the endzone on another draw. He burst through tackles like a madman. The corner from UCLA makes a spectacular shoestring tackle coming up from an angle. Now State's side was going crazy and the UCLA side was silent and seemed to be in utter shock, including my girl Sabrina. There was only ten seconds left in the game and State called a timeout. T looked exhausted. After the timeout, State came back out. The crowd was going crazy. They again handed the ball to T on a power play and he goes in the end zone, untouched, with only two seconds left on the clock.

The score was now 24-29. State decided to go for two. On the play, they fake the fall to T and he dives over the top; meanwhile, the quarterback tucks the ball and runs into the end zone on a naked bootleg. State was now ahead 24-31. State then squibs the kick-off. UCLA gets control of the ball and a couple of players pass the ball to each other until one gets tackled, and the game is over. T jumps around with his teammates, celebrating their upset victory. In the midst of this, T comes over to us and we celebrate with a big group hug. Shea and I are downright proud of our boy.

I stop in the middle of our celebration and look across the field. My eyes couldn't believe it. Sabrina had her arms around the UCLA star running back, and she stuck her tongue deep down his throat. Shea then looks across the field and T also turns around to look across the field. They see the same sight as me. My heart started to flutter faster than a hummingbird on crack. T and Shea just looked at me as if to say "Man, I'm sorry, dog!" But I had to remain strong. I told T "Fuck that. This is your moment. Let the celebration continue, my nigga!" We talked a little more shit to each other and then T had to go and talk to reporters and go shower. We told him we would see him back at the hotel and he said, "Alright, I love ya'll niggas. I mean that shit." We replied, "We love you too, nigga." Then Shea turned to me and said, "Do you want to go over there?" I said, "No."

Then, we were on our way back to the hotel. We finally got back to the hotel. We put all of our things into our bags and then T came in the door. He looked at me and said, "Are you sure you're alright?" I said, "Yeah, I'm cool." He then said, "Well fellas, I'm on my way out of here. Ya'll call me when you get back home."

Shea and I both say, "Alright, boy." We all gave each other pounds and hugs, then T left. Shea and I gathered our things and went downstairs to check out the hotel and get back on the road. The ride back home was fairly silent. Shea and I talked about how T got off and how proud we are of our boy but other than that, conversation was barely present. Then out of nowhere, Shea says, "So what you going to do about Sabrina?"

I tell him, "Well, now I have to put her in another category. She was once an angel to me. Now she's nothing more than my broad at UCLA." Shea replies, "Are you going to tell her what you saw?" I tell him "No. I can always keep that as my ace in the hole. I just have to think of how I'm going to play this. But one thing I'm not going to do is, I'm not going to up jump and do something I might regret later. Shea then says, "Well, after all this shit and seeing what you saw, what did you really learn about yourself and Sabrina?" I replied, "Well, I learned whatever you do comes back to you one way or another, and life is a mothafucker. As far as Sabrina goes, she was doing nothing more than being a young woman away from home for the first time." Things then got quiet and Shea and I enjoyed the silence all the way back to the bay.

Rumor Mill

The first thing I did when I got home was call Belize. I guess this was typical. I just had my little heart crushed by one girl so I had to run to another. It was so funny, how my last thoughts of Sabrina before I actually saw her were angelic and now every time I pictured her face it had horns, and she was donned in a black cloak fully equipped with a pitchfork. Since I told Belize pretty much everything she asked me, "Did you expect to see anything else?" I had to respond, "No, I pretty much got what I expected to see, but expecting to see it and seeing it are two totally different things." From there, we talked about school and when the next time I planned on seeing Sabrina would be, since I was so crushed from my trip. I assured her that I was quite alright, and would prove so the next time we saw one another. She just said, "We'll see."

I told her we could hook up the next day and then she said, "Oh, I almost forgot to ask you. You know this girl named Terry?" I was like, "Yeah, why? What's up with her?" She said, "Well I heard she was from around your way and I just wanted to know if you knew her." I was like, "For what? I never ran up in her, if that's what you're thinking. She's fucked more niggas than the law allows." Belize says, "Are you sure you never fucked her?" I say, "Yes! Why? Who told you some shit?" She says, "Willie, it's nothing like that. I just wanted to know, because word on the street says she's HIV positive." I was like, "What? Dizamm! Well you ain't even got to trip because I ain't ever ran up in that." Belize says, "Ain't one of your boys named D-Luv?" I was like "Yeah." She then says, "Well a lot of people seem to think she might've gotten it from him." I replied, "Hell No! It's a lot of people out there hatin' on my potna. They got his name twisted up on some bullshit. She didn't get that shit from my nigga!" Belize replied, "Don't get mad at me. I'm just telling you what people are saying. I don't know anything about the situation. This is strictly what my girls were telling me." I told her not to listen to any of that nonsense, because that shit wasn't hardly true. We both agreed we wouldn't be going to school the next day, and we would meet at her house for the slap and tickle session. After I got off the phone with Belize, I called Shea. He told me I should get to his house in a hurry. I asked him why, but he just told me I should just come over.

I had to holla at my moms for a minute. She's steadily asking me if I saw Sabrina on my trip. I tell her I don't really want to talk about it. Mom just gave me this funny look and said, "Alright." I told her I would be going over to Shea's house and I would be home later; she tells me not to be coming in too late, and I'm off on my journey down the railroad tracks.

On my way down the tracks I start to think of what Belize said. I really had to go through my memory bank and make sure I didn't run up in Terry on one of my late-night adventures. I knew I didn't, but I had to go over it thoroughly in my mind because although I never had any type of sexual relationship with Terry, I know if the opportunity would've occurred I just might have. The thing about it that was so sad is that no one would've been mad at me if I did.

She had the reputation for being a slut but every guy that ran up in her understood why the other did. She was a tall chick with mediocre looks and an ass that wouldn't quit. This in itself wasn't too bad but it was the way she dressed and talked that just took her to hoe status.

She would always wear the tightest pants you could ever imagine. You cold see her lips a mile away, and I'm not talking about the lips you speak with. Speaking of the lips you talk with: this girl had the filthiest mouth you ever heard. She would talk about sucking a dick like you talk about going to the sink and getting a glass of water. I know D ran up in her a while back, but I heard she started really sleeping around more recently. I really didn't know why I was thinking of it so much, since I know my boy D was cool, but things just pop up in your mind from time to time. Between thoughts of my boy D and still thinking about Sabrina, I got to Shea's house pretty quick. This is why I didn't mind walking to his house. It always gave me time to reflect. As I walked up to Shea's door, I could hear a gang of niggas inside loud talking. When I knocked on the door no one could even hear the damn thing. It sounded like the people in the background of Marvin Gaye's "You Got to Give It Up."

All you heard were a gang of mumbles and grumbles in different conversation. I knocked, or should I say banged on the door this time. All of a sudden you couldn't hear much on the other side of the door. All the conversation stopped, then I heard Shea say, "Who is it?" I reply, "It's me, nigga. Open the door." Shea then opens the door and says "Damn nigga, we thought you was the law, out here knocking like you done lost your damn mind." I reply, "Man, I was out there knocking for about an hour before ya'll niggas graciously decided it was time to answer the door."

Shea just gives me a look like, *whatever, nigga.* "I'm glad you're here, so you can get a load of this shit." It was a full house. Our entire little secondary clique was pretty much there. There was our potna

Butkis. We called him this because he was a big ass nigga, with a big ass butt and some fat juicy ass lips. Thus, the name Butkis. There was D-A, also known as Dark Angel. We called him this because he was a dark-skinned dude, but he was also a genuinely nice guy. There was our potna Water Boy. We called him this because he could down a forty ounce of beer faster than anyone in our clique. Our potna White Shit was also in the house. We called him White Shit for two reasons. One was because he was so light skinned that he looked like he could pass for white. The other was because he looked so much older than he really was, he reminded us of that old shit that would turn white after months of sitting on the lawn. Our potna who would drop in and out of the scene was there. His name was TNT. We called him this because he would gradually get drunk during the night and all of a sudden, "Boom!" He seemed like his high went from a calm cool manner to an explosive aggressive type of high, where he would be roughhousing everybody.

Sandals was also in the house. There was no particular reason why we called him this. Well, I take that back. He looked funny and the name was funny. Also, one day he came through Shea's in the ugliest pair of sandals you'd ever seen and White Shit said the sandals he had on looked like the sandals Jesus wore when he walked across miles in hot desert. I guess this is why we called him Sandals. And finally, our potna Voltron was in the house. We called him this because he would transform so much. All of these niggas was in Shea's house talking big shit about rumors on the street. There was one big one going around right now. It seemed as though my girl Belize, was on top of this one.

Shea tells White Shit, "Man, tell Willie Wood what you've been trying to tell me, boy." White Shit turns to me and says, "Man, word on the street is your boy D-Luv got that shit." I was like, "What? Man, how did motherfuckers come up with this old crazy shit?" White Shit says, "Baby named Terry got that shit and she told the people at the clinic that she thinks she contracted it from a guy name Darrell Ray. Now, if I'm not mistaken, that is that nigga D-Luv's given name." Sandals just blurts out from nowhere, "Man, that nigga ain't got that shit! First of all, he ain't gay. Second of all, he ain't all skinny and fucked up looking, with sores and shit all over his body." Butkis then says, "How do you know? Have you been fucking the nigga lately? When is the last time you saw that man naked?" Water Boy then says, "He does have a point. Have you been secretly fucking the nigga or what?" Everyone then starts to laugh. Dark angel then says, "Man that shit really ain't all that funny. If that boy does have that shit, what do you think his momma is gonna go through losing her only son and better yet, what do you think that man is thinking right now. Shit he could be like, 'Fuck it, I want to kill myself' or even worse he could be like, 'Fuck the world. I'm gonna fuck everything, in sight'."

Then, I reply, "Damn D-A, you always have to be the one to think like a grown up and shit. Fuckin' with you nigga's might start to grow a conscious. In any case, niggas just need to stop gossiping like some hoes. We don't know what the fuck is going on. What if this broad Terry is mad at D for some shit that happened between the two of them and decided to twist his name up? What if she really believes D gave this shit to her and it's really some other nigga? You just don't know." TNT then chimes in and says, "Man if that nigga got the shit. I wouldn't be surprised because he done fucked everything this side of the Mississippi and if he doesn't I wouldn't be surprised because the motherfucker ain't gay. So far the only mother fuckers I know with that shit is either gay or shoot-ups."

Then here comes Voltron with his crazy ass comments. He just yells out of nowhere, "Well, that nigga is definitely a candidate, because I heard he likes shooting his wee-wee up in breezy asses. If that ain't a gay tendency, I don't know what is." Everyone just looks at him like they want to slap the shit out of him, and continues the conversation, tuning him out quickly. Either way, D's name was hot in the streets for all of the wrong reasons. Whoever got this ball rolling with this Terry girl better hope they never get found, because I know if D or his cousin or any of their potnas found out about the origins of this rumor, things could get real ugly, real quick.

Everyone went into their own little groups, talking about why they thought or didn't think D had that shit. It was like a circus. Shea and I had our own little side bar. Shea came over to me and said, "What do you think?" I just said to him, with my shoulders hunched, "I don't know, man. I just got off the phone with Belize before I came over here, and she told me that she heard D had that shit." Shea dropped his head and said, "What? This shit is definitely out there, then. Belize ain't really too much in the loop and she heard this shit. Something bad is going on, man." I told Shea, "Look. Neither one of us has hollered at D yet and we don't really know what's up with him and this broad Terry, so until we talk to this nigga, let's just kick back and assume that this shit is false and defend our nigga to the fullest." Shea just looked at me with a look of confidence and said, "Yeah, you're right man. We gotta hold it down until this nigga surfaces and let it be known that our boy is cool."

We gave each other a pound and a hug then went back to join the other cats in the house with our newfound confidence and squashed all the bad talking about D, and moved on to the next subject. Shea's girl Cynthia came in the door with a bag full of groceries. All of the niggas in the house greeted her at once, "Hello Cynthia." She said hello to everyone in the house and went straight to the kitchen. Shea followed her into the kitchen. You could hear them arguing over something, but it sounded like one of those petty arguments that wasn't going to turn into anything big. They basically both were adamant about the points each one of them were trying to make and the other was reluctantly agreeing.

So, after their conversation in the kitchen, Shea came out smiling, and Cynthia started to cook. A little time went by and all of a sudden, like you were being slapped in the face by your moms after you said a bad word, the aroma just hit you. I asked Cynthia, "What the hell are you cooking?" She replied, "Jambalaya." All of the niggas in the house instantly started looking like wild, savage wolves closing in on a baby gazelle. They looked just like cats, you know how they are when they see something good and they instantly start salivating. Everyone looked savage except for Shea. He knew this meal was being cooked for him and he acted like he couldn't even smell it. Butkis looked at Shea and said, "Bruh, is the niggas gonna get a chance to taste that shit or what?" He said this low enough so Cynthia couldn't hear him, but loud enough so the rest of us could. Everyone had this look on their faces like, "Damn, I'm glad somebody asked because I'm hungry as hell". Shea just looked at Butkis and said, "How did I know yo' big brown rhinoceros looking ass was gonna ask me about that shit? Just hold on a minute. After she cooks the shit she's gonna go to school, so just wait until she leaves and then we'll try to make it happen chubb-rock." Everyone breaks into laughter and Cynthia gives us the curious look like, "Hmmm, what the hell are they laughing at?" We go back to talking about what's going on in the streets, besides the rumor going around about our boy. It seems as though he's not the only one who might be stressing about this Terry chick.

Supposedly she has married men rushing to the clinic to get tested. Other ballers in the town have supposedly gotten tested and suddenly disappeared. Many people seem to think those cats tested positive and went to another part of the country to spread their deadly news.

I was getting tired of all of this talking about HIV and AIDS. The shit was too depressing for me and besides that, I was doing too much fucking to have the shit on my mind that heavy. It was getting late and I didn't feel like robbing Cynthia's pot anymore than I already had. I think I had one bowl and shit was it good, but Butkis and the rest of the bandits were going nuts in the pot. Shea regulated at the last moment, so there was some left for Cynthia, but after sweating over the pot in front of all of us, I knew that wasn't going to be enough for her. It was just another argument waiting to happen for her and Shea, so as much as Shea was changing, some things were still the same. I told Shea I was about to hit the road and he offered to give me a ride down the street, but I told him I needed some time to clear my head and walk off the alcohol, so I was going to walk down the tracks. He asked me if I was sure I didn't want him to give me a ride and I assured him that I would be alright. I gave him a pound and told everybody else that I was out.

My first thought after I left Shea's and started walking was, "I can't wait until the next day, when I'm supposed to hook up with Belize to get my freak on." I had to stop and think to myself, "Damn, you just got through talking about HIV and AIDS and the first thing you think about when you leave is fucking." Typical nigga shit. I didn't want to walk down the train tracks at this time of night because there were no lights and you couldn't see a thing, so I decided to take the streets to the house. It was a fairly cold night out, and I wished I had accepted Shea's offer for a ride. I made my bed so now I had to sleep in it.

As I was walking down the street, I kept noticing how the distance looked a lot longer to the house than my usual route via the train tracks, when all of a sudden I noticed a car creeping up on my right hand side. I turned to get a better look at the car, which was a '68 Cougar sittin' on some gold ones, and I heard a voice say, "Give me some cho-cho." I was like, "D? Is that you?" He responded, "Yeah it's me, nigga. You need a ride to the tilt?" I immediately shouted, "Hell Yeah!" I quickly ran over to the passenger door and hopped in. It was nice and warm inside D's car. He asked me, "Nigga, when are you gonna get yo' ass something to ride in?" I responded, "My school is a twenty-minute walk away. My potnas' kick-it crib is fifteen minutes away. All my hoes have cars and I always got scrill in my pockets, so I ain't trippin. My world is spinning rather nicely."

My nigga D said, "Damn I never looked at it that way. I guess you alright then. Me personally, I could never be without something to ride in." I asked him, "When have you ever seen a nigga who is supposed to be ballin' walking?" We both looked at each other and laughed. D asked me if I was in a hurry to go home and I really wasn't, so I told him,

"No." I was a little tired but my boy was on my mind, so I decided it would be worth the lost Zzz's to catch up on some things with him. D had a forty he was sipping on and he offered me some. I had just come from drinking and smoking with Shea and the rest of our potnas, so the last thing I wanted to see was a drink or a joint., so I told D, "Naw. I'm cool. I just came from Shea's and we been drinking and smoking all night." D just gave me this weird look and say, "I guess that means you don't want to hit the jay either?" I was like, "Naw man. I'm cool."

D fired back, "Naw man, you ain't cool!" I was like, "What the fuck is wrong with you?" D, replied, "Man, I know what you been hearing that punk shit about a nigga up in these streets man, and you can't even drink after your boy no more. You can't even hit the jay no more. What's up wit' that? You think your boy go that shit?" I was like, "You know what, nigga? I just spent the last two or three hours defending your paranoid ass to some gossiping ass motherfuckers, and you gonna come at me with this punk shit! Nigga, give me the damn forty! Give me the shit! I'll drink the motherfucker just because, dammit!" D looks at me and grasps the forty back and says, "Naw, man. It's cool. I apologize for trippin' on you like that, but I know what niggas is saying about me. I can't take this shit anymore. I know the shit ain't true, but I see it in niggas' eyes when they holla at me! My true folks get at me about it and I set the record straight, but these degree of separation niggas give me funny looks. I think I might have to smoke one of these niggas to set an example." I tell D, "Look. Fuck all these other dudes. If you know it ain't true and all your support system know the shit ain't true, that's all that matters. Time will tell the rest of these niggas what's really the truth."

D responds, "Willie, that's easy for you to say, but when it's a rumor going around like this about you, that shit is hard to shake. Hoes don't want to fuck with a nigga no more. The same niggas that used to share beer with me all of a sudden don't feel like drinking when I'm around. Even the punk ass police make little comments to me when they are shaking niggas down like, 'Don't worry about him, he won't be around much longer' or 'Don't cut that guy, if he bleeds on you we might as well call you a priest'. This shit is really fucking with my mind, Will!" As always, D finds a way to blow my mind with the stories he would tell. However, this was the first time I could remember him telling me a story and looking like he wanted to cry. I felt funny even thinking this, but I told D, "The only advice I could really offer you is to pray."

"Whenever I get to the point when I feel all of the walls are closing in on me, I fall to my knees and pray." D just looked at me and said, "You know what? That's the best advice anyone has given me yet. All the other advice I had been given, niggas was telling me to beat somebody down or just outright kill mothafuckas. I knew coming to see you would even me out." I gave D this funny look and he said, "That's right. I was coming to holla at your square ass Wood. You got this special quality about yourself that niggas like to cling to. Don't ever lose that quality, man. Always be yourself and you'll make a lot of people happy."

With that, we were pulling up to my house. D says, "Alright man. It was good hollering at you, man. I needed to chop it up with someone with a pure heart. Do you need any scrilla?" With that, D pulled a wad of c-notes. I was like, "Damn! Boy what the hell you doing with all that? I appreciate the offer, but naw man, I don't need your scrilla." D was like, "Yes you do." He then stuffed the wad of money in my jacket pocket and said, "I really would consider it an insult if you tried to give me that money back. Now get out of my ride." I gave him a pound and said, "I'll holla," and D was off in the wind.

It really made me feel good that my potna thought so highly of me. I can't even lie though. It made me feel a lot better when I got done counting the cash before I went into the house. My boy slid me seven G's without blinking twice. As I went into the house and hopped into bed, my final thought before my head hit the pillow was, "Belize could thank D for this tremendous fuck session she's going to receive in the morning, because my dick is so hard with joy right now it could break through ten-inch marble".

Shea Day

It was really amazing what the next three and a half years brought by Shea, ,me, T and D were still headed in the direction many people thought we would go in. I had transferred from the local junior college after achieving my Associate Arts degree, to the local State College and was working towards getting my Bachelor degree in Sociology. Shea climbed the ladder at Taco Shell and became a supervisor. Even he finally realized that he was low-balling himself and decided to take a couple of classes at college. While attending college, Shea met with a recruiter from UPS and got hooked. Shea started working at UPS about two years ago and he's still complaining about lifting those heavy-ass boxes.

I've got to hand it to him though. When we first graduated from high school the expectations for my boy were very low. He's proven over these years that he's not afraid of hard work. My boy T blossomed into a nice running back. After his freshman year he was considered as one of the backs to watch in the future and over the next few years he didn't disappoint.

My boy was an honorable mention All-American in his sophomore year, and in his junior season he was first team All-American. T started getting all kind of press going into his Senior Season. He was a preseason All-American. Many publications had him picked as their player of the year and many had him picked as the Heisman Trophy winner.

T was doing it bigger than any of us thought he would. Even D came down with us to catch a couple of games. Speaking of D, my boy was in and out of jail for the last three-and-a-half years. I would see him on the streets for a minute and the next I would be getting a collect call from county.

The first couple of times he would call me collect, I started thinking what my phone bill would look like, but since he shot me so much scrilla in the past I didn't say a word. But to show you what kind of dude he was, when he got out he would always come by the house and drop me off a couple of hundred dollars. I would always tell him I didn't need the money, but D would insist that I take the money. The rumors of him having AIDS died down to a low whisper. People saw that he still looked healthy and nothing about him changed much, so everyone just figured he was alright. The female that supposedly said D gave her this deadly disease just fell completely off the map.

I would ask some of the females who used to hang with Terry if they knew where she was, or whatever happened to her and they all would say, was she just moved and didn't tell anybody where she was moving, or they just didn't know where she was and they weren't thinking about her. So I just threw it to the back of my mind and didn't ever try to dig it out.

Going in and out of jail only increased D's rep. He had an electric personality, so he would meet cats from all over the bay and they would see how people treated D and his cousin, so he just became larger than life all over the bay. He always had that asterisk next to his name because of the rumors, but people still treated him with much respect because of the way he carried himself.

Over the years, Belize and I became somewhat of an item. Neither one of us planned on things turning out this way, but things just kind of crept up on us. She changed her major to business administration and graduated from U. C. Berkeley in the top ten percent of her class. She had a cool job making a grip, and we were just clicking on all cylinders. Sabrina and I sort of weeded our way out of our relationship. I sweated her for about another year or so after I was devastated during my trip to L.A., but eventually her dude dogged her out. She started fucking around with other cats out there to get dude jealous, and before you knew it, she became a household name for all the athletes out there.

She did try to come back into Willie World, but Belize had her beat in every way, fashion, or form. I mean, the main reason I got with Sabrina was because she was supposed to be my square chick. She was smart, going to college and came from a rich family. Now that I was with a female who already graduated college, had her own money, looked way better and could fuck like a champ, I no longer had use for Sabrina.

The natural course of life had made her become extinct in my world. It was Darwinistic. She just couldn't evolve with me, so she fell by the wayside. Besides all of that, I decided that fucking as many females as I could was no longer a goal of mine. All of those rumors about D slowed me down considerably. Belize knew how I was when we met, so she never questioned me about how many females I was seeing but I told her she never had to worry about me fucking around. I really meant it, from the bottom of my heart, but the dog in me always made me chase the cat every now and again. I was just a lot more selective these days and they all took a back seat to Belize. I had to take a good look at what I had.

She was beautiful, intelligent, and the sex was off the hook. She always would look out for me. When she'd be out shopping with her friends, she would pick up something for me. If she thought I would look good in it, it was just natural instinct, she would just get it for me. She would cook for me. If I left clothes at her pad, she would have them washed and neatly folded when I came through. She was just on point with everything.

It took Shea pulling my coattail to really make me appreciate what this young lady was doing for me. One night we were having a conversation about women, and I told him all of the things Belize was doing for me and he just looked at me and said "Nigga, what are you waiting for?" I replied, "What do you mean?" Shea said, "Man, this girl has a lot going for her and she treats you like she's your servant when she's the one who can afford the servant. You need to recognize and lock that up, before she realizes the same shit I realize." I asked him, "What do you realize?" Shea replied, "I realize that you are one of those niggas who expects that kind of treatment from all breezys you fuck with, therefore you don't really appreciate what the hell this breezy doing for you." I just stopped and took in what Shea said. I said to Shea, "Damn I think all of those Gorilla cookies you ate are finally starting to pay off. The protein from the banana flavoring is starting to affect the thinking in the right side of your brain." I stopped and waited for a laugh but there was none there. Shea was dead serious and he just looked at me and said, "See what I mean?"

I looked back at him and said, "You know what? You're probably right, but I don't think anything is wrong with me expecting to be treated like the player I am, and before you go giving me that look again, what I mean is, I present myself in a manner that makes females treat me the way they do. It's their choice to present themselves the way they want to be seen. If one wants to spoil me, shit it's all good. If she doesn't and she's not too intelligent or doesn't have much else to offer, she gets treated accordingly. I have a lot of respect for Belize, baby boy, but because of the way she came in I have to be cautious. After all the first night I met her, I fucked her after I fucked her potna and she knew, so that's what I'm dealing with." Shea looked at me and said, "I see your point Willie, but all I'm saying is maybe she was just so sprung off of something about your stankin' ass that it made her do something out of character. That shit does actually happen every now and then. Most breezys be lyin' when they say 'You're so special that I did it for you,' but some really do mean the shit. Since your episode ain't nobody ever seen or heard of her with another dude. She's told you that she hasn't been with anyone else for the past four years, so maybe there's something there for you to contemplate."

I looked at Shea and said, "Point taken. I haven't gone into it and broke it down as much as you, John Madden, but I've thought about all of that before. Believe me, she gets dap for playing her part." With that, our conversation ended. Ever since Shea and I had that conversation, I put my relationship with Belize on another level. I wasn't thinking marriage or anything like that, but more respect was due and rightly so given. I suppose a lot of this came from Shea, because he was headed in a more responsible direction in his life.

I remember a time when this dude would give up on anything if it required him to do any work, or thinking for that matter. A lot of cats that we hung with would crack little jokes about Taco Shell and UPS, where Shea works, but they can never crack too hard. He always had clean clothes, a car to ride and he kept his girl Cynthia fitted too. Shea and his brother were getting along great. Every now and then big Jess would join us when we hit a bar. There wasn't as much kickin' it at Shea's anymore with his new-found sense of responsibility, but the times we did kick it, it was more intense now. On the weekends, when Shea didn't have to work, it would be like a mad house at his pad.

Jess started to spend the weekends at his old lady's house more since Shea showed he could handle himself more responsibly, and we would have a ball. Niggas would come through with alcohol and sticky green and just have a good time, and there would never even be a hint of a fight breaking out. Even though we started to gain a greater sense of responsibility with working and going to school, there was nothing like kickin' it on Friday and Saturday nights.

This was the only time traces of the old Shea would show up. On one particular Saturday night, things got a little too wild for everyone's taste. Shea and Cynthia were getting into it fairly badly. Shea was upset because he gave Cynthia some money to pay a bill and she wound up being a little short on money after she got her hair done, and she had to take some of Shea's bill money to cover the costs. Shea went to go use his telephone and it was cut off. He used his brother's phone to call the phone company and cuss them out, but they told him the bill had not been paid. So when Cynthia came home from getting her hair done, Shea asks her, "Did you pay the phone bill?" Cynthia replied "Don't be mad at me." Shea says, "Mad at you for what? I just asked you one question. Did you pay the phone bill?" Cynthia replies, "No, but I can explain." Shea says, "Explain What?" Cynthia interrupts, "I was getting my hair done and when the girl finished with my hair and I went to pay her, I realized I was 150 dollars short." Shea yells, "150 dollars short! There no way in hell you went to the shop to get your hair done and realized after the fact that you're 150 dollars short. What you did was said, 'fuck me,' and saw another more expensive hairstyle you liked and decided to get that shit!"

Cynthia snaps back, "No I didn't. I just went a little over budget, that's all. Why you trippin' so much?" Shea fired back, "Why am I trippin'? Why am I trippin'? I'm trippin' because I gave you 300 dollars to pay a bill now my fuckin' phone is cut off. On top of that where's my damn change?" "Cynthia gives Shea back a hundred dollar bill.

Shea says, "Where's my other fifty dollars?" Cynthia looks at him and says, "I put fifty on the phone bill." Shea gives a sarcastic smirk, looks and me and says, "Willie can you believe this bitch. I give her three hundred dollars to pay my phone bill, and she comes back with a hundred dollar bill and pays fifty on her bill. If that ain't the dumbest shit I ever heard in my life, I don't know what is." Cynthia, enraged at Shea, yells, "Motherfucker, I know you didn't just call me a dumb bitch, you raisin-dick bastard! Don't get to actin' crazy just because you're in front of your friends, nigga! They gotta go home sometime dammit!" Shea hollers back, "Oh, now I'm raisin dick huh? You wasn't saying that this morning when it was all in ya mouth. Then, only thing you was thinking about then was raisin nuts? And who the hell made you fuckin' Tony Montana for a day, you talkin' like you about to whup up on somebody when my boys leave or something. We both know that ain't going down, so don't front in front of the company."

I refrained from laughing, although I wanted to badly. This thing was getting ugly fast. Cynthia said, "Next time pay your own motherfuckin' bills and you won't have to worry about this shit." Shea says "Obviously. Next time I'll leave a trail of cheese, so you could follow it directly to the pay center." Cynthia's eyes began to well up and she said, "You know what, nigga? Fuck you and everything you love! A bitch make one little mistake and you treat her like she done murdered your momma. I'll bring by all your shit tomorrow because I ain't taking this shit no more. Fuck You! I don't ever want to see you again. Oh yeah, Bye Willie." With that she left and slammed the door behind her.

Shea just looked at me and said, "Can you believe that bitch, nigga? She spends my scrill and got the nerve to be mad at me. Fuck it. I'll worry about her ass later. Let's go to the store and get some drink boy. I need to get fucked up. And you know what really trips me out about the whole thing?" I answer, "What?" He asks, "What was she about to do with the other hundred dollars? I mean, she put fifty on the bill and kept a hundred to the neck. What the fuck was she thinking?" I just say, "I don't have a clue, man," in a somber tone. And with that, we hopped in Shea's ride and got to the liquor store.

We headed toward our usual spot on the corner, which has all the malt liquor you could stand and the coldest in town, if I might say so myself. We get to the store and I'm leading the way inside. I look behind me to ask Shea what he wanted and he wasn't behind me. Shea had stopped at the counter, where all the hard alcohol was kept. I asked Shea, "What the hell are you doing over there, boy? You know you can't handle that hard shit." Shea just looked at me and said, "I'm gonna handle it tonight, boy! This bitch done pissed me off and I need to get fucked up, and fast. I might as well put this hundred dollar bill to use, ya know." I started thinking to myself, "Oh shit. If I don't regulate this nigga's alcohol intake tonight, we could be in for a woozy."

I walked over to Shea and asked him, "What are you talking about getting?" He looked back at me and said, "A fifth of that one five one." I was like, "Ah hell, naw! I'm not trying to scrape your ass off the ground tonight nigga!" Shea replied, "Fool. It's supposed to be a gang of niggas coming through tonight. So I'll probably barely even get to put my hands on the shit." Still skeptical, I was like, "Alright, but I'm gonna be watching your ass all night. If I see your ass remotely starting to turn your human ass into a mermaid and try to swim in this shit, I'm cutting you off the juice, playa." Shea replied, "All that won't be necessary. I'll have my couple of shots and be done with it. I'm a grown ass man, nigga." With that we both put in half and got the fifth of one five one. I had to get a case of brew too. Just so I could have something there to get my boy off the hard shit in case he started to get out of hand.

We get back to the house and settle back in. We didn't immediately start drinking the Bacardi because we wanted to wait for a couple of cats to come through, so we started off drinking the beer. I knew my decision to buy the brew would pay dividends. About an hour and a half passed by, and the doorbell rang. I was a little closer to the door than Shea, so I answered it. I opened the door and to my surprise, it was our boy Camel, who we didn't see too often. We called him Camel because he looked like the Camel on the ad for Camel cigarettes. He was the blackest, coolest white boy you would ever want to meet. I opened the door wide and was like, "What up cam-dog? It's been a while since niggas done seen your pale ass. Ah, and I see you brought some lovely partying gifts with you, huh?" Camel came in laughing and said "My jungle bunny potnas, I come with peace offerings from the superior race." He, Shea and I busted up laughing and then immediately turned our focus to the two snow bunnies Camel had with him. Shea and I looked at Camel like, "What's up?" And Camel gave us the look back like, "Once again, it's on." So Camel came in with the two snow bunnies and introduced them to us. One of them was named Heather and the other one was named Tiffany. We knew off the bat that Heather was with Camel because she clung to him like white on rice.

She was decent looking. She looked to be about 5 feet 5 inches tall, dirty blonde hair, about a 36 C, and of course no ass at all. This isn't really what we would come to expect from Camel, seeing as he usually dated only black women, but every now and then he would dabble.

The other chick, Tiffany, looked a little more like what a brotha might want to hit. She stood about 5 feet, 8 inches tall. She had short black hair, a big somewhat sloppy ass and she looked to be about a 38 DD. They came inside Shea's and settled in. Camel told us he was

looking for our potna Terrell, because Tiffany was supposed to hook up with him and they would then go on a double date, but Terrell had hooked up with another female and told Camel he wouldn't be available until later on in the evening. There was a hotel across the way, and Camel said the females got a room there because they didn't want to drive all the way back to Modesto that night. He invited Shea and I to come over there and kick it. Shea and I looked at each other like a couple of couple of wild wolves in the presence of a wounded lamb, and said, "Hell, let's raise up out of here before niggas start to trickle in."

Shea grabs the fifth of one five one. We grab our jackets and we're out the door. Camel asked as if we wanted to squeeze in the car with them, but Shea and I declined. We knew if we were gonna do any dirt on this night we would need a separate getaway car. So Shea and I hop in the car and follow Camel and the breezys to the hotel. Shea and I were talking in the car and we made it clear to one another that whoever Tiffany chose would be able to do his thang without the other interfering. It was also understood that if someone did hit' em the other had the green light to try and get his on next. So the table was set. I agreed to these terms for several reasons – the most important of these reasons being, Willie World always gets the woman. I had supreme confidence that this female would wind up jocking me and then I could set the table for Shea.

We pull up into the hotel and Camel lets the girls go ahead of him, and meets us for a quick huddle. He rubs his hands together as if he's the quarterback about to call a play and is like, "Niggas, I got a case of brew on ice in the room and some sticky green, so the party is gonna last all night. Shea then pulls out the fifth and says, "Oh, party we shall." Camel says, "Where did ya'll niggas get that? I know we didn't stop by any stores." Shea tells him, "I brought it from the house. Willie and I boughtit earlier and I think it just might come in handy tonight." Camel just looks and us and says, "Well I know at least one of ya'll is fucking tonight because baby is a big ole freak, so to whichever one of ya'll that hits I know it's gonna be a lovely night. To the other, don't be mad damn it, just let the night unfold. Who knows? Both of ya'll might get lucky tonight." We follow Camel up the stairs and to the room.

It was a double occupancy room with a nice big round table towards the bottom of the beds. Camel brought some dominos with him, so we flip a coin to see between Shea and me who's going to watch and wait until someone loses. Camel flips the coin and Shea calls tails. The coin hits the ground and Camel says, "Heads it is. Sorry Shea, I guess you have to play spectator while I tax these nigga's asses. I look at Camel and say, "Yeah right. Daddy 'bout to show you how to count the dots on these mothafuckers." So Shea takes the one five one and grabs everybody's cups and says, "Before anyone gets to do anything, we all have to take a shot." He pours a shot into everyone's cup and we make a toast. Camel tries to set the mood and I give him much dap for that. He says, "To everyone being open-minded tonight, and if you feel like getting freaky do it, because it's all in the family."

Shea and I look at each other as if to say, "Good job wetto. Now let the games begin." Both of the snow bunnies seemed at home in our presence. Neither one of them acted funny style in any way, shape or form, so we assumed they were cool with Camel's toast. Everyone took their shot and we started playing dominos. Shea had the fifth in hand

and sat on the bed. I told him, "I'm watching you with that drink, boy. As a matter of fact, does anyone want a beer? I'm about to get me and the boys a beer to sip on." Everyone said they wanted a beer, so I play host and go get everyone a beer. Shea looked at me and gave me a sarcastic look as if to say, "Oh, that's how you gonna get the bitch tonight, huh? Make me look like the irresponsible lush while you mediate right into her drawls." I gave him a look back, which suggested saying, "Nigga please, I'm trying to help us all out, because it you get too drunk its lights out for all of us." I handed him his beer, passed beers around to everyone else, and we started our game. The game started going just as I suspected. I came out of the gate whoopin' everybody's ass. I could see Camel wasn't even trippin' though. He seemed content on having a good time. He and Heather would go back and forth making fuck faces and Tiffany was riding my nuts hard. Every joke I told, she would laugh.

Even the bunk ones kept her in stitches. I kept catching her staring at me, and I would ask her "What's wrong with me? Do I have something on my face or something?" She replied, "What? You don't like it when women look at you or something?" I said, "I don't mind, as long as she has good intentions." She said, "Well maybe I shouldn't look at you, then." I say, "Why not?" She says, "Because right now, all I have is bad intentions in store for you." Camel looks at me and says, "Damn. I think I might want to hop in your shoes right now. Shit, you got the best hand in the house tonight." Heather looks at Camel and says, "I don't think so." She then starts to rub her hands across his crotch and Camel's eyes roll to the back of his head. I then look behind me to see what Shea is doing and the boy is knocked out. I look at the bottle of one five one and see that it is half empty. I say, "Oh shit, my boy done drank half the liquor and passed out." Tiffany just looks at me and says, "Well, do you want to fuck him, or join me in the bathroom. I need help unbuckling my belt." I look at Camel and say, "Don't come in the bathroom for about 45 minutes to an hour." He looks at me and says, "If I have to go that bad, I'll go outside. Go do your thing, boy."

Tiffany grips me by the hand and we go into the bathroom. She immediately sticks her tongue down my throat. I closed the door behind us as we enter the bathroom. I try to cut the lights on to see what I'm working with, but she immediately turns them off. We continue slobbering all over one another as we tear each other's clothes off. I start kissing her on her neck so I could halfway focus on getting her bra strap undone. As I complete that mission, her breasts just fall out like, "Ah, free at last". I bend down a little and start licking her breast as if I were an infant starving for nutrition. This really seemed to turn her on, because she was moaning like I already stuck my little wee-wee inside her.

Things started to progress as she went down and started licking my chest nipples. I hadn't really had a female concentrate so hard on this area of my anatomy. She was sucking and licking them with her mouth and tongue but as she was doing this, she started squeezing them with her fingers. I was like, "Wow!" This was another notch on my Freaky levels belt. This was the first time a female ever stimulated me so much without fondling my penis. Just as it started feeling real good she went down and pulled out ye old Snickers bar. She seemed like she started to bob her head up and down before she actually put it in her mouth, because it was all one continuous motion. She just took control of my shit as if she owned it.

She gave what my potnas and me like to call "hard head". We called it "hard head" for two reasons. One was because she seemed to be working so "hard" to please my "head". The other was because when a female is going up and down on your dick with her mouth like a jack hammer it just seems appropriate to call it "hard head". This little gift of Tiff's came complete with surround sound, sound effects. It sounded as if she started sucking a tootsie roll from start to finish without ever swallowing the juice until the very end. The exceptional thing about this was it sounded like this every time she went down on my dick. All I kept thinking in my mind was, "Damn, this shit feels good and I hope she doesn't expect the same in return because it just ain't gonna happen." I could hear Camel in the other room say, "God damn. She sounds like she's trying to suck a watermelon through a speaker wire." He then lets out a loud laugh and I could hear his girl Heather say, "Shut up" in a low toned voice. I couldn't take it anymore. I just pushed her away from my dick and I told her to turn around. She does so, as if her life depended on it. As soon as she turns around, I look at her round ass through the darkness and I kept seeing a flashing neon light in my head that kept blinking with the words, "Insert penis". I was like a little kid fumbling to get out of my school clothes to go out and play. I finally find the wet spot and in I go. There was no resistance. I felt like I had just dipped my dick into a beaker filled with hot molten lava. She was so hot and wet, it was ridiculous. The whole episode was a thing of beauty with one exception.

This girl was screaming as if a nigga was stabbing her frantically with a thousand spear tips. At first this was a big turn on. I mean when the dick first went in she made a nigga feel like he was shoving a stick of dry salami with the length of a ruler and the girth of a can of Campbell's soup in a hole the size of a thimble, but after about fifteen minutes straight of that shit, you feel like you want to gag the bitch with bandana.

Although the sex was feeling good, I had to end this session before its time. So I start pumping like a mad savage, which makes her yell louder and more rapidly and then I pull out and dump my load all over her back and hair. It was a pretty intense session we just swung, so I lost my legs for a minute and I had to sit down. We had our little weird "after the sex is over" conversation, which wasn't actually that bad. She told me about how she came up here with the intentions of meeting our potna Terrell, which I already knew and had no problems with, and how she was glad we met, but she still wanted to see him. I let her know that I didn't have a problem with that, and in fact he was my older potna and I'm sure that if he knew what went down, that he wouldn't have a problem with it. She didn't know if that would be the case, but she was glad I wasn't trippin'.

The thing I knew and she didn't, was that Terrell was out with his main chick that he was still in courtship with. Which means, he'll probably take her out for dinner and then a movie. After which, he'll take her home and give her a kiss on the cheek and tell her he'll call her in the morning. Seeing as how he hasn't boned this girl yet and doesn't plan on it for a while, after he drops her off he'll be horny as hell and he'll come over here so he could take his sexual frustrations out on Tiffany and dig her out. Me, myself, I had my main girl Belize, so I wasn't trippin' at all either., so we come out of the bathroom to total darkness.

We could hear the mixture of Camel and Heather's moaning, groaning and kissing, along with Shea's loud snores. It was a weird sound, since Shea was sitting at the domino table with his head on the table, knocked out. Tiff and I go and lay on the other bed. We were not even in there for five minutes when there was a knock at the door. I go to open it up and low and behold, it's my boy Terrell. He looks at me with the expression on his face as if to say, "Camel told me everything, it's all good."

We gave each other pounds as he starts to enter through the door. He quickly assesses the scenery and is like, "What up Camel?" Camel sticks his head out from under the covers and says, "Nothing, you big inner tube lips motherfucka. Can you please close the door? A nigga is sweatier than a motherfucka and you got me exposed to the world at large and its elements with the door wide the hell open." Everyone lets off a laugh and Terrell closes the door.

He goes over to Tiff and says, "What's up girl?" She says, "Nothing," with her face turning cherry red from shame. After this they continue to share small talk and idle conversation, until I hear from Terrell, "What's up? You gave my nigga some love, so you can't fuck with me?" She says, "I didn't say that. I don't have a problem if you don't." I didn't mind what was going on at all. The only real problem was, I was still on the bed with these two. I saw Terrell jam his tongue down her throat and I was thinking, "Brotha man. You really don't want to do that. My dick was just embedded in there," but they kept going at each other. The next thing you knew there was penis insertion. I could tell because Terrell let out this sound as if he were dipping his penis into hot lava, just like myself earlier, and Tiff started again. It sounded like the police turned on their sirens inside the room. So, here we are. Camel getting down in one bed. Terrell getting down in the other, with me in the same bed and Shea sleeping at the table. I know God had to be looking down with tears in his eyes. I think we were covering a good share of sins in that room that night. I felt even weirder because Terrell kept looking at me while he was doing his thang.

He was smiling and making faces and shit. I tell you, it was just downright weird. About thirty to forty-five minutes later both Camel and Terrell were done. We turned the lights on and everybody caught their second wind. When we turned the lights on, Shea finally decided he wanted to wake up. He woke up with his eyes as wide as golf balls as if to say, "Where the hell am I?" He quickly realized and his eyes went back to normal size. He looked at Terrell and said, "What up, boy?

When did your big lip ass get here?" Terrell looks back and says, "Long enough to see your ass slobbering on the table for an hour." Everyone is wide awake and it's about four in the morning. Camel looks at Shea and says, "We thought you was done for the night, party pooper."

"I told Willie to go and get your warm bottle and a bib." Everyone in the room begins to laugh. You could tell Shea didn't appreciate this at all, but instead of going into an angry tirade he just says, "Ah nigga. I was just getting my second wind. Where's my cup?" He reaches over and grabs his cup and begins to fill it with the one five one. From there, the party started up again. We began to drink, play dominos and listen to music. Apparently there were people in the hotel who really wanted to sleep, because the hotel manager came up to our room and told us if we didn't keep it down that we would be kicked out. At this time, everybody was feeling good so we more or less told him to fuck off. With that he walked off and said he was going to call the police. When he said this we started hooriding him, calling him every name in the book. After he disappeared we started to assess the situation. Three drunken niggas, one drunk white boy who thinks he's a nigga and two drunk white girls. We instantly said, "It's time to go."

Everyone went inside the room to collect their belongings. As we were leaving, Shea looked at me and said, "Willie, did you fuck the white bitch?" I answered to him, "Yeah. Why, what's up?" He passes me his car keys and says, "Here. Go wait for me in the car, I'm about to fuck this bitch real quick." As soon as he hands me his keys and turns around, he runs right into Tiff, who was listening to our whole conversation. She quickly says, "Who are you gonna fuck?" Shea looks at her rather sheepishly and says, "You." Terrell, Camel and I burst out laughing and then I look at the table. There stood an empty fifth of one fifty one and six empty cans of beer where Shea once sat. I started thinking in my head, "Oh my God. This nigga done turned into the Werewolf of London."

Meanwhile, Shea isn't making much progress with convincing Tiff that she's going to fuck him and we start to file out towards the cars. We get to the parking lot and now, instead of Shea talking about fucking this girl, she's becoming all kinds of white bitches, hoes, and tramps. Well, she gets to the point where she can't take it anymore, and she swings at Shea and hits him in the head. Wrong move for her. Although he was extremely inebriated, he's a man and she's a woman, so he regains what little bit of composure he has and pops her upside her head.

After he does this, Terrell flies in with his cape real tight and says, "Man, why you gotta be hittin' on girls, nigga? Don't be mad because you can't get no pussy, coward!" To this Shea says, "Coward? Nigga I'll get' em up with you too." Right at that moment, Shea swung at Terrell and it was like the punch was in super slow motion. It caught Terrell completely off guard, so he didn't have a chance to move. Shea's punch came up a little short, but it was just long enough to catch Terrell in his bottom lip. I promise you this was the most hilarious thing I'd ever seen. Shea's blow came awkwardly from over the top, so when it hit Terrell's lips, it was like he'd just flicked them as if to say, "Now what, nigga? That's just a prelude slap to some bigger and better shit."

The girls, Camel and myself couldn't help it. We all burst out laughing. This was bad for Shea. You could tell he was drunk out of his mind, and Terrell was just slightly on tilt. It was as if the laughter incensed Terrell even more than the blow. We always gave him grief about his big lips, so Shea's flickering blow might as well been an overhand right from a skilled boxer. Terrell then just charges Shea and threw him into some nearby bushes. Shea went flying like a quarterback who had been blind-sided by Lawrence Taylor. Instead of Camel and I going to check on Shea, we both charged Terrell. We were jamming him up because he knew Shea was drunk out of his mind and we felt he could've handled the situation better. Neither one of us were thinking of what we could've done to defuse the situation but hey, when drunk minds get together, things like this happen. After we get done jamming Terrell about his behavior and convince him to apologize for his actions we turn around and Shea was gone. It was like some *Twilight Zone* shit. He just disappeared. We all started yelling, "SHEA!" SHEA! Where the hell are you?"

By this time the sun is coming up and the hotel manager is warning us that the police are on their way. We're not paying much attention to him, though. All of a sudden Heather says, "There he is." We look across the street and all we could see is a Shell gas station. Terrell, Camel, and I are like, "Where?" She says, "Look. There on the ground." We look and we see Shea laid out in the middle of the gas station. He's lying there on his back next to a guy pumping gas in his car. We start yelling, "SHEA, what the hell is wrong with you nigga! Bring your ass over here!" All of a sudden, Shea looks at us and says, "Noooo!" He looked as if we were body snatchers trying to come invade his mind or something. After he yelled at us, we start to cross the street to come and get him, but when he sees us coming, he jumps up and starts running. Shea ran the opposite direction, at the same time he begins yelling, "No, No, No!" I started thinking, "Oh my Goodness, this nigga done flipped his wig." Just when I thought this and didn't need further confirmation, the nigga ran through a wooden fence. Camel, Terrell and I looked at each other like, "Ah hell naw! We got to get this nigga fast."

Camel and I followed Shea through the fence while Terrell went around to try and cut him off. When we went through the fence it looked like we were trailing a tornado. We were now in a residential area and Shea had gone through clothes people had hung to dry in their back yards and kicked over little kids' toys. Man, it was just a disaster. To further complicate things, this nigga kicked in someone's back door and ran through their house. Camel and I were looking at each other like, "Oh shit." Camel ran through the house and I ran around the front, attempting to catch Shea. Camel came around the front and said, "He's not in the house." Just then, a big Hillbilly came out the front door with a twelve-gauge and says "What the hell is going on? Do you motherfuckers wants to die?" We just look at the cat and say, "Look, mister, our friend isn't feeling too good and we're just trying to get him before he gets into any trouble. We apologize for the inconvenience." At that, the Hillbilly says, "Inconvenience? Inconvenience? You young motherfuckers. Ya'll lucky that I wasn't getting no pussy or he didn't wake up my daughter, otherwise you bastards would already be dead. Now go get that crazy asshole because the next man might not feel as generous as I do right now. You little cheese-face fuckers." With that the Hillbilly turns around and storms back into his house. Camel and I look at each other and just shake our heads.

Then, in the distance, we could hear a loud thumping sound. We look down the street and saw Shea kicking someone else's front door. Before you know it, we're in hot pursuit. We start running down the street shouting, "Shea! Shea! What the fuck is wrong with you, nigga?" As we get closer, Shea turns his attention to us and shouts, "No!" He immediately breaks in the opposite direction. Unbeknownst to him, Terrell was right there waiting for him. Terrell does his best football impression and just tackles him. Terrell was significantly bigger and stronger than Shea, but on this day Shea had nutty strength or something. I mean, it was just like the movies, when you have to kill the psychotic killer five times before he dies.

Terrell could not hold this boy down. He looks at us and says, "What the hell are ya'll looking at? Help me dammit!" Camel jumps on the ground to help Terrell hold Shea down. I told them I was going to the hotel to get Shea's car. I asked Terrell how he got to the hotel and he said he had one of his potnas drop him off, so that was a good break. All we had to do was get one car and tell Heather and Tiff to follow me in their car, so I get back to the hotel and tell the girls what's up. They hopped into their car and followed me.

When I drive up on Camel and Terrell, they look like some fathers who are disgusted in their promising young son. I roll up to them and they stuff Shea into the car like they're stuffing luggage into a trunk. Shea is screaming all the while, "Stop! You're hurting me!" We all say in unison, "Shut the Fuck up!" By this time, we were all cranky. No one has gotten any sleep, we had a gun pulled on us, we had to hunt down this nigga and on top of everything the hotel manager had already called the police on us. The only thing on our minds was getting Shea's ass to his house.

As we're driving this nigga, Shea keeps yelling, "Willie! Willie!" In a drained, totally disgusted voice, I respond, "What's up, nigga? Stop calling my name if you ain't got shit to say." After this, he just keeps saying, "Where will she go? Where will she go?" When I first heard this, I thought he was just repeating one of the songs he liked to listen to a lot by Babyface called "Where Will She Go?" It wouldn't be too unusual for a person in a drunken stupor to be singing out the crack of their ass, but just to humor myself I ask Shea, "Who? Where will who go?" He then blurts out, "Cynthia! Where will she go, Willie?" Man, my heart just dropped to the bottom of my stomach. I was like, "Nigga, your ass went fuckin' nuts over this girl you was just treating like shit, and acting like you didn't give a fuck about? You had niggas damn near get killed over a broad? You know, you need your ass kicked. If you wasn't so fucked up already, I would've slapped the shit out of you. As a matter of fact, why don't you take this with you." And with that, I gave Shea a quick slap to the cheek.

Then I continue, "Now take your ass to sleep, so when you sober up and wake up I can kick your ass." With that, Shea started nodding off and so did Camel and Terrell. I was left to drive home with my idle thoughts. This was the last time Shea really acted an ass. He has come a long way since that night, but whenever and I mean whenever he gets too far out of hand all I have to do is say is, "Ay man, you remember that night you went crazy?" And all jokes stop. A lot of people inquire about what happened that night but we chose to keep that a secret. Camel, Terrell and I swore to it.

Things were still moving along quite nicely for my boy T. He had a banner senior season and was named conference player of the year. He didn't win the Heisman Trophy. Most people believed he would to do something tremendous to get if anyway. There was this big 6'4", blonde–haired, blue-eyed quarterback from Texas University who was getting all the publicity before the season started. Even though T-Bronze ran for 1,600 yards and caught fifty passes for another 570 yards, people figured the white boy would get it just because, and they were right.

I was a glossy-eyed youngster, so I just knew they couldn't deny my boy, but they did. It was O.K., though. The sorriest team in the NFL just drafted a quarterback the year before and now they were looking

155

for a running back, so T was assured he would be the number one pick in the draft. With this news embedded in his mind, T decided not to even go back to school after his team won their bowl game, and he ran for a record 355 yards.

T was never the one to delve too deep into the books but I figured he had to be pretty close to achieving his degree and he would love to get that for his moms, but he wasn't trippin'. He would later tell me that he rarely went to class and sometimes he went so infrequently he expected to be ineligible a couple of times, but a C or B would mysteriously show up on his transcripts from classes he never enrolled in.

He would also later confess that he spent most of his college days at his new girlfriend's dorm room. Her name was Tracy. T-Bronze was never one to really stress females but Tracy was one I couldn't fault his sweating. She was a true brick house. She was 6'0 tall, and was a member of the school track team. This women didn't have an ounce of fat on her body. She had it all, nice calves, full lips, beautiful white teeth, perfect breast size and she was a straight A student. Most of all she was a genuine woman. My boy T wasn't the sharpest tool in the shed, but he was very logical and he could be as smart as he wanted to be. He just chose not to max out his smarts because he was more of an athlete than a thinker. As a result of this, I thought Tracy might have been one of those females that figured she can go ahead and get with a dumb athlete, marry him, divorce him and get half of his loot, but when she and T were together they looked like two old friends seeing each other after being away from each other for a while. This was cool, my boy T. If this woman Tracy had a plan she sure was cold and calculated about it, because she knew all of the right moves and she had us all fooled. Shea and I fell in love with her instantly, but the time D went with us to see T play he said he couldn't say too much about her because she seemed too good to be true and you know what they say about something that seems to be to good to be true. D always brought a dose of reality into the equation.

T was happy, so I was happy for him. I told him, I wished we could've graduated from our respective University's at the same time, but since he was about to be in the NFL, I couldn't pass judgment.

The way I see it, we both went to college to make a better life for ourselves and our families, and he was about to be in a far greater position to do that than I would. Meanwhile, Shea dipped and dabbed in his books enough to be getting his AA degree from the local community college around the same time I was graduating. It was kind of funny seeing Shea go through his metamorphosis while the people who doubted him and sat back on the same street corners, drinking the same beer and ridiculing him for working and going to school, had to now give him dap for achieving his goals. Amongst our little circle it was like a chain reaction. T got his scholarship, so I knew I had to go to school.

Shea saw me go to school, so he knew he had to work and eventually go to school. Now the niggas hugging the corner by the liquor store are starting to notice it ain't as cool being there anymore and they're starting to either step up the hustle or get a job. These are only the smart ones, of course. There will always be some cool nigga who has convinced himself that he'll never work or pay dues to anything. I've come to learn that these will be the same niggas in front of the store ten years later begging for quarters or dollars.

For the most part, Shea's parents had dropped out of the picture. It was a sensitive subject with him, so none of us really brought it up after he let it be known that he didn't want to talk about them. His brother Jessie was enough family for him. In his own way, Jessie would let Shea know that he was very proud of his accomplishments.

He would cap on Shea, saying things like, "Boy. I remember when there was a time when I thought I was gonna have to be giving you change in front of the liquor store, and now it looks like you might have to be giving me change in front of that mothafucker. Naw, I'm just kidding, but I'm damn proud you got your shit together. You even made me step my shit up. I Love you, little brah." He would be so sincere when saying this, but upon exiting the room he'd make a comment like, "Now don't you little niggas eat all the food in the fridge" or "Don't fuck up the house while I'm gone, I just cleaned it you little niggas." He would say this just, so we don't think he's getting too soft or something, but it was cool because we understood.

Meanwhile, I was in the process of getting my Bachelors degree in the spring. With everything going on with T and Shea, I kind of got lost in the mix because it was like everyone figured I was going to graduate and get my degree. If it weren't for the excitement of both of my parents, I probably wouldn't hold too much stock in what I was doing myself. My moms was so overjoyed that her boy was graduating from college with a 3.2 GPA. My dad was also a proud camper. When I would go visit him he would have all of his boys over and say thing like, "See this is the proof of my genius. My boy came out of his momma blind to the world and we raised him to be the level of graduating from a four-year university with honors. If that don't prove it to ya'll, then I don't what will." In return, his boys would say things like, "Luckily for your son, he had a smart momma," or "That only proves your son's genius, to come into the world hindered with a daddy like you and still succeeding and going to college must've been hard on the boy." They would usually share a good laugh and then my pops would tell me how proud he was of me and how he wished he and moms were still together, so we all could share this as a family, but I would tell him that things work out the way the do for a reason and it didn't lessen the joy of the occasion. For me it was actually a blessing in disguise. It really doubled the joy of the occasion.

When I was at home with my mom, we would celebrate in our own way and it was totally different from the way my dad and I celebrated. My moms was more upbeat and joyous about the occasion and my dad was more realistic and cerebral. Moms would rejoice in the occasion or in that particular moment of the achievement, whereas dad would be more like, "O.K. We've jumped this hurdle, now it's time to jump the next." Both worked for me because it kept me balanced.

Belize was still very much in my life, as was Cynthia in Shea's. Things were moving along rather systematically with Belize and I, so I saw no reason to mess things up. I slowed my role down considerably as far as messing around with other chicks, because I realized I had a good one already. I think Shea came to the same conclusion. He also slowed down and paid homage to the woman Cynthia was. As a result of us doing a lot of things together, Cynthia and Belize became close friends and hung out with each other, even when Shea and I weren't around. At the first thought of this, the both of us were scared shitless, but since we both slowed down as far as our extracurricular activities, it was actually a plus. Now when Shea and I wanted to hang we could just bring the girls along. When T was in town even Tracy hung out with us, so it was all good. We all got to hang like the old days and the girls got to be close to us and have their own little pow-wow without anyone being upset or offended.

Meanwhile, over in my boy D's world, things were starting to heat up tremendously. He and his cousin Vell had a solid hook-up for getting their dope. There were rumors floating around about dudes getting robbed and killed during their exchange and it had some guys spooked about who to trust. Since D and Vell had been dealing with the same Mexican cats for about five years, they weren't too worried. They also felt safe because during the time these other cats were getting robbed and killed, they had made maybe four or five buys themselves without anything looking the least bit suspicious.

The good thing that came out of this for D and his cousin was nobody else had any dope. None of the other D-boys trusted anybody else, so they all started buying their dope from Vell and D. Now Vell was buying big weight from their Mexican potnas, who in turn warned them that they were getting hot. They told them that they rarely hung in the hood, but when they did they heard their names ringing constantly. D and Vell took it in stride because they felt no one they were dealing with had enough heart to take their money, life or dope. I heard a couple of the dudes who hung out in front of the liquor store talking about how much money they thought D and Vell were having and when I would go to Shea's house that's all anyone would be talking about. Since we didn't hang out with D too much anymore, we didn't really know what was true and what was false, but what we did know, was that we needed to holla at him soon. I've always known D and Vell to be on top of things, but maybe a little reiteration from his square potnas will definitely keep him on his toes. Another negative that came out of this was D and Vell had to deal with a lot of dudes who they really didn't know and a lot of dudes who they knew were jealous of them. No one actually knew exactly how D and Vell got all of their dope but there was a lot of speculation.

Some people heard of the Mexicans they were dealing with, but couldn't confirm this, because D, Vell and Nino never told anyone and the Mexicans they were dealing with didn't want to supply anyone but Vell in that area, so their names wouldn't be hot. Then you had people who speculated it was D and Vell who were killing everyone else and sewing the market up for themselves. Some would explain this logic by saying Vell was a savage already and since D supposedly had the virus he didn't have anything to lose. With these rumors floating around it made it harder to deal with some of the shady characters they had to interact with.

One night things went from bad to worse in a hurry for D. Late on a Friday night, D got a call from his cousin Vell, telling him he wanted to meet him and Nino at the spot so they could go handle some business. D immediately wants to know what kind of business, because if it had to do with dope they wouldn't usually get down if things weren't set up in advance, but Vell said he didn't want to talk about it over the phone and he needed D to rush over. So D, who was comfortable at the house, rushed to get dressed, hopped in his car and was on his way. On the thirty-minute drive a lot of things were going through D's head. He didn't know if his cousin had a beef with someone or if he wanted to do business with someone, or what the deal was. His pager kept going off with the same 800 number and a 911 behind it. He didn't think it was his cousin, but since he was getting close to the spot he didn't bother calling.

D finally arrives at the spot and he sees his cousin and Nino, and he asks his cousin Vell, "What's up?" Vell says, "Baby boy, I got a nice jolt for us." D replies, "Yeah, nigga. What?" Vell says, "Do you remember that cat who kept buying two kilos every other week from us from the Westside?" D replied, "Yeah." Vell says, "He had been telling me he was going to expand his operation and now he's about to head out towards Texas and he wants all fifteen kilos from us."

D replies, "Damn. What kind of deal did you cut him?" Vell replies, "I only took five hundred off each key." D replies, "Shit that's all good, but I have a couple of problems with this shit cuz…" Vell replied, "I know what you're going to say already. I thought you never did business wit' niggas from the West side of town? You know I normally make dudes meet us halfway, but since he's been a good customer and he's copping so much, I thought I'd do him this one solid. He also has a plane to catch tonight in Frisco so I think of it as good customer service." D says, "Man, cuz I got a weird feeling about this one. It's going to be a lot of dope and money in unfamiliar Terrytory." Vell says, "Don't trip. I had Nino check the park where we're meeting at already. I told dude we're going to meet at a specific place in the park and Nino got the spot where he's going to be hiding out perfectly placed in case the funk jump off." "Alright, man." D says, "If you think it's cool, cuz, I gotta roll with you. Just remember, if anything and I mean anything starts to look funny, we're up outta there blazing."

Vell says, "Don't even trip like that, man. Dude is cool. He's been buying from us with no hassle and now since he's stacked his chips he's trying to expand his operation, it's all good for everybody. Besides, this one big sell right here will put us closer to where we want to be: out of the damn dope Game. And you know if this nigga even think of doing some weak shit, his ass is out, ya know?" D replies, "Yeah, you're right man, fuck it! Let's do it. Oh Yeah, was you paging me before I came over here?" Vell replies, "Not since we talked on the phone." D says, "Man, somebody's been paging me off the hook." D looks at his pager and says, "I'll be right back. I'm going to make a quick phone call at the pay phone." Vell hollors back, "Make sure you make it quick, girlie, time is of the essence." D says, "Fuck you, nigga! You know it's only going to take a second."

D rushes across the street to make his phone call. He really has no idea who it is, because the number looks so unfamiliar, but he figures it's probably one of his little breezys telling him she wants to hook up with him for the night. D reaches the pay phone and dials the number. He hears the voice on the other end say, "HIV and AIDS hotline. How may I help you?" D says, "Hello?" The female voice once again says, "HIV and AIDS hotline. How may I help you?" D says, "I'm sorry, I dialed the wrong number." At this time, D's heart was racing like a hummingbird on crack. He redialed the number on his pager, making sure he looked at every number and dialed it carefully. He pushed each button with the preciseness of a brain surgeon. After he dialed the number, it seemed like it was taking forever for the person on the other line to pick up. D started to feel a little better, because he felt there was no way, if it really was an HIV and AIDS hotline, that no one would answer. But right when he was about to hang up the line, he heard a deep male voice say, "HIV and AIDS hotline. May I help you?"

Meanwhile, across the street, Vell and Nino were like, "Hurry up nigga. Let's go handle this!" D's mind was being pulled in a million directions. He was wondering who the hell would page him to an HIV and AIDS hotline. Was it a dude hating on him because he fucked his girl or something? Was it some female he wronged in the past? My man didn't have a clue. In order to move on and deal with the task at hand, he had to just write it off as someone hating on him, because he knew he didn't have that shit. After all, he still looked good, still had his appetite and he never got sick, and it had been quite sometime since those rumors about him circulated.

After this one quick minute of brain storming, D-Luv brought his heart rate back to normal. He ran back across the street, and joined his cousin and Nino. Vell asked D, "Who was that paging you boy? Was it one of your late night hypes?" D replies, "Man, it was just this broad trying to check up on a nigga and be all in the business." Vell says, "Speaking of business, let's go handle ours." With that, D, Vell and Nino loaded into Vell's car. They dropped Nino off around the corner in his underbucket and were on their way. D turns to Vell and says, "Cuzzo, how are you feeling about this one? I don't mean money-wise. I mean your gut feeling."

Vell says, "You know what cousin? I'm a break it down to you like this. I'm a soldier about mine and I know Nino is a soldier about his, which means neither one of us is scared to die chasing this money. For the longest time I had my doubts about you, but over the years I've seen you manifest from a nigga who had the potential to go all out, to a nigga who's been going all out. I have a funny feeling in my gut about this shit but fuck it. It ain't the first time I've had this feeling and it might not be the last, but I know this is big money and if I don't get it somebody else will. Besides that, cuz, I wouldn't bring you nowhere with me with the intentions on getting us killed. The truth of the matter is, I feel like can't nobody touch us when we're together. You got this shit inside you that you don't even know yet, so don't be scared on this ride. Just go at this shit like business as usual and let God decide when it's your time."

With that said, D just looked at his cousin and said, "Fuck it man. Let's make it happen." It was a silent car the rest of the ride; you could barely hear the Spice One tape playing in the background. It was almost like it was backdrop music to their scene. Either that, or it was just down low so D and Vell could hear themselves think. They rolled up to the park where they were supposed to meet. They drove around one time just to check the lay of the land.

Everything looked cool, so they went a block away and parked. They saw Nino's underbucket on the same block, so they knew he was already there. Vell told D to grab one of the bags in the trunk so they could make their way to the park. D asked Vell, "Why are we only taking half of the shit, if you trust dude and you want to make this deal so bad?" Vell replies, "I never said I trusted this nigga and even if I did trust him, I would only bring half the shit and let things transpire from there anyway." Just then, D went from his cool "let's make this deal" mode to "fuck, I hope there aren't any more surprises" mode. They both tucked their nine-millimeter handguns in the small of their backs and were on their way.

They both walked up to the park, scanning the terrain for anything looking suspicious. The dude they were supposed to meet was in the back of the recreational center like he was supposed to be, and they could see Nino not too far away in the shadows. It was actually a great hiding place, because if you weren't looking for him there would be no way you would ever guess he was there. D and Vell walked up to the dude and Vell greeted him with a pound and dude was like, "Who is this you brought with you?" Vell says, "This is my partner. I told you I had a partner in this business and I never make a decision without him." The dude says, "I remember you told me that, but when we made this deal, I was under the impression that it was gonna just be me and you here, considering the fact that I'm buying so much weight and I wanted to be on the under in regards to what I'm trying to do." Vell says, "Don't trip, this is my peoples and anything that goes down here stays here. If you don't feel comfortable about this or anything like that we'll just take our dope and you can take your cash and we'll go our separate ways. No harm, no foul, ya know." The dude says, "We're here now, so let's go ahead and make this transaction and be on our way."

Vell says, "Show me the paper." The dude says, "Here you go." He opens the bag and it's full of cash. D looks at the cash and then he looks at Vell's reaction. The reaction in his face didn't look like that of a man who was happy with what he just saw. Vell looks at the dude and says, "Man. It looks kind of light right there, playboy." The dude replies, "Well, this is a big transaction, so I brought half the cash on me and left half the cash in the car, just in case." Vell tosses the dude the bag of dope and says, "I guess great minds think alike, huh, because I only brought half of the dope with me and left half in the car." The dude tosses Vell the bag of money and they both share a sly laugh. Vell then says, "Are you ready to make the other transaction, so we could be out?" The dude says, "Yeah. I'll just signal to my boy to bring the rest of the cash and you could send your peoples to the car and everything will be everything." Just then, dude backed out of the shadows and entered a lighted area and made a hand motion to a car across the street. He then said, "the rest of your money is on the way." Vell looked at D, and D knew Vell wanted him to go to the car.

As D was leaving, he could hear Vell say, "Oh, you thought I was supposed to be coming alone and you brought your boy with you huh? What's up with that?" D heard the dude stuttering into an explanation, but he was busy thinking about going to the car and getting the rest of the dope so they could get out of there. On the way to the car, D noticed that Nino was no longer in the same bushes he was hiding in. D just chalked it up to Nino probably moving to another spot so he could be in better position should something go wrong. As D approaches the car, he sees someone walking toward him. The person was walking on the same side of the street and headed directly at him. This person wasn't walking in a suspicious manner, so D didn't feel threatened. When the person got close enough he flashed a cigarette and asked D if he had a light. D let this person know he didn't have a light and the guy started to walk off. As D got to the trunk of the car the guy turned around and said, "Hey are you sure you don't have a light?" As he was asking the question he was walking hastily towards D. D closed the trunk and replied, "I told you I didn't have a motherfuckin' light, nigga. Raise the fuck up out of here."

"Now what the fuck is up?" As D is saying this, he's backing away from the guy and pulling his gun from the small of his back. As the guy was going towards D, he exposed a knife he was carrying. D yells at the guy, "Put that damn knife down, nigga. What the fuck possessed you to come to a gunfight with a knife anyway? You smoking or something? You damn village idiot! Put the knife down and kick it towards me!" The guy then slowly places the knife on the ground and kicks it towards D. Then D asks the guy, "Are you with them niggas in the park?" The guy nervously replies, "Yeah, but man, it wasn't my idea, man! Please don't shoot me!" D yells at him, "Shut the fuck up! How many of you niggas are there with you?" The guy replies, "Two more. We were just going to get the dope, man! We weren't going to hurt anyone!"

D yells back, "Nigga! If you insult my intelligence one more time, I'm gonna put a fuckin' hole in your head! If you expect me to believe you were gonna tickle me with that damn knife then you're sadly mistaken, you dumb motherfucker. Now turn around and don't make no sudden moves because if you do, I hope you kissed your momma before you left the house tonight, because you ain't gonna see her again." With that said the guy turns around and asks D not to shoot him again. D tells him, "Shut the fuck up and walk. And I'm going to tell you this: if anything is wrong with my cousin or my potna Nino, you're a dead mothafucka."

As soon as D says this, the guy turns around and lunges towards D, similarly to how Cornelius lunged at D when D committed his first murder. And just like then, D was put in a situation where he could do nothing but pull the trigger. This guy wasn't as big as Cornelius, so his momentum didn't cause him to land on D. The force of the bullet caused him to veer to the side of D. D goes up to the guy as he's taking his last breath. D leans over and says, "Why the fuck did you do that, nigga? I told you I wasn't going to do shit to you, unless ya'll fuck with my cousin." The guy looked up to D and said, "I didn't kiss my momma before I left the house tonight, but I did fuck my baby's momma and kissed my son good night. Now the question you need to be asking is if your cousin and your other potna kissed their mommas, because I guarantee you they done suffered the same fate as me." After he said this, the guy's eyes rolled into the back of his head and he went to his eternal resting place.

D turned his attention toward the park and started to run furiously. As the park comes into view, he could see two dudes kneeling over his cousin Vell's body, savagely stabbing him. D yells out "No!!" And he raises his gun blasting all the way. The two dudes hear D yelling and the hear the gunshots and start running immediately. As they try to run away D runs behind them trying to line up his shots. Boom, Boom, Boom, Boom. D shoots until he empties his clip when he's done, there are two bodies on the ground at the parks edge D rushes to his cousin to see if he could save him. "Vell! Vell! Are you O.K. cuzzo?" D asks. Unfortunately for D, there was no reply. His cousin lay in a pool of blood, lifeless. Off to the night of his cousin, in the bushes, D could see Nino, lying on the ground, lifeless also. With tears in his eyes, D ran towards the two lifeless bodies at the edge of the park. One of the two guys had the bags of dope and money from the meeting, and D quickly collected them both. He went across the street to the dude's car, popped the trunk and got the other bag of money.

D ran as fast as he could back to the car with all three bags. Once he got into the car, he was so nervous that he thought his cousin still had the keys. He hops out of the car and starts running to the park, when he realized his cousin gave him the keys, so he could get the rest of the dope. In mid-stride D stops to go back towards the car but then he thinks this was a sign to go see his cousin again, so he turns around and runs back to see if his cousin is alive. D returns to the scene and sees his cousin lying exactly how he left him. He kneels down, kisses him and tells him he loves him. With that done, D runs back to the car.

As he's driving away his pager starts to go off again. D looks down expecting to see the 800 numbers to appear once again. This time it's not an 800 number but the number did have an unusual area code. As he's driving to the secluded Hotel where he and his cousin picked out to change clothes if something went wrong, his pager keeps going off. Once he gets to the room, he calls the number. A woman answers on the other line, "Hello." D says, "Did somebody page?" The female says, "Yes. Is this D-Luv?" D says, "Yeah this is me. Who is this?" The female says, "Damn. That's a shame you been through so many females, you can't even recognize my voice." D is growing impatient by this time and he says, "Look. I don't have time to be bullshitting. I've just been through some serious shit, so state your name and business because I'm about to hang up." The female voice says, "O.K. nigga. This is how it's going down. This is Terry and I tested positive for HIV some time ago, and I'm now full-blown with AIDS, and get this. The kicker is I've never done drugs and I've never been with a gay man. When I found out I had the shit, you were the only one I was sleeping with, believe it or not. Is that stating my business enough for you?" D stood in silence with his mouth wide open. Terry says, "Are you still there?" D says, "Yeah. I'm here." She then says, "What do you have to say for yourself?" D says "Nothing." He then hangs the phone up. With his heart beating so rapidly, D had to lie down for a moment and collect himself. He lies in the bed and puts his hands over his face. He notices his hands are wet when they touch his face. When he looks at his hands he sees he has blood all over them. He gets up and goes to the bathroom to wash his hands. As he is washing his hands he notices the blood keeps coming out. He looks further and sees he has a nice sized cut on his hand. He then wraps it in a towel and proceeds to change his clothes. All the while he's doing this, his pager is continuously going off. He looks at his pager to check the number and sees it's Terry. He then turns his pager off and continues to clean up. I then get a phone call that night.

D tells me he needs a friend to talk to and he needed to talk right now. I told him to come on through, even though it was an ungodly hour in the morning. After what seemed to be no more than ten minutes, but was probably more like thirty minutes, I go outside to talk to D after he honks three times, and I can't believe my ears. He told me everything that went down. I couldn't believe it when he told me about Vell and Nino. It was one thing to know the fate of most people who deal in the game of drugs, but when it's somebody you actually know, it all of a sudden makes the names you read about in the newspaper turn into living, breathing people, instead of black ink on white paper. Then when he told me about Terry, I damn near died. I asked him if he thought she was bullshitting and he said, "No." Right then, all of the rumors and D's sexual behavior flashed in front of my eyes in a split second. I told D, "You have to get tested now, man."

D said, "I know, but I'm scared as hell, Willie. I've never felt like this in my life. I feel like I've been killed two times tonight." I told D when my times get their toughest, I just pray. D then gave me this funny look and I told him, "I'm not saying I'm the most religious person, but I do know that God exists. I love and acknowledge him and when my times get rough, I pray. It always works for me. Whenever things don't make sense and I feel like I can't go on, I give him a call. It sounds like you need to give him a call right now man." D said, "Man, that's about the only thing I've heard tonight that makes sense. It's funny, I knew after all of this went down tonight, you were the only one I could talk to that could make any sense of this. Go back to sleep, man. I apologize for getting you out of bed. I'll holla at you later, man." I gave him a pound and went back in the house and hopped into bed. I said a quick prayer for him and went back to sleep.

Say It Ain't So

The day after the shootings in the park, it was all over the news. "Four victims found slain in local park," and one victim's blood was all over the headlines. The whole town was buzzing with rumors. I felt like the gatekeeper to the truth of the matter. I told Shea and T what D-Luv told me. I knew the truth would not leave our circle, no matter how many times people asked us questions about it. Everything was still a blur to me, but as the days went by and turned into nights, things began to clear up for me. The police started to make sense of the murder scene. They found Vell's gun and two knives in the park and one knife near the other victim around the corner. "It's like a scene out of a slasher movie," said one of the detectives.

They had no definite leads but they said they were sure that someone else was there on the scene and either positively witnessed things from a distance, or survived slayings themselves. As more days started to go by, the detectives made a statement saying they found evidence that proves there was another suspect on the scene that was loose in the public. They said there were five total victims that night, but they found six blood samples. They encouraged whoever was the sixth person to turn himself or herself in, because it was just a matter of time before they would catch him or her. When I saw this I wondered what must have been going through D's mind.

I didn't have to wonder long because he called me at the house. He told me he was dropping out of sight for a while and he would be in touch with me from time to time to find out what was going on.

Meanwhile, I was praying to God the police wouldn't connect me to anything and ask me questions, because I didn't want my name on any transcripts that would hurt my future. Besides that, my parents would be extremely hurt if they found out I was mixed up with this in any way. As stupid as it may sound, I felt obligated to be there for my friend, no matter the cost. D-Luv dropped out of sight and I started hanging at Shea's a lot more. In my little world, I had a couple of things going on. I just graduated and didn't have a clue as to what I really wanted to do with my future.

I was never a guy who thought I was going to college to take certain courses to go into a certain profession. I just knew it was the right thing to do if I wanted to get ahead in society. Belize was starting to talk about marriage, which really blew me away. My first thought at the mention of the "M" word was "Damn, am I grown now? Please somebody tell me quickly, because if I am, I don't want to be yet. I still feel like I can't make the decisions grownups need to make." One night after chillin' at Shea's proved to me I really wasn't ready.

I told Shea I was ready to go home, and as usual he asked me if I needed a ride and I said, "No," as usual. It was kind of late, so I took the streets instead of taking the tracks, so I'm walking along minding my own business, when I hear this voice say, "What's up, baby? I'm slumming tonight. Can I give you a ride?" I turn to look and it was none other than Sabrina. My heart gave a quick flutter and before you knew it, butterflies were dancing in my belly like a two-year old baby on a sugar rush. I say, "Sabrina, is that you?" She leaned out of her window and said, "What other female looking this fly is creeping in the ghetto, looking for you?" We both just looked at each other and laughed. She said, "Well, are you just going to stand there, or are you gonna ride with me?" I replied, "Well, I think I should walk home. It might be a little safer than going home with a stranger." I started to walk and Sabrina's car creeps slowly in the dark night. She shouts out of the car, "Look boy! You know I ain't no stranger, and the only reason I would be on this side of town is to see your ass, so can you please hop your black ass into my car?" I reply, "I guess I can let you back into Willie World for a second." She replies, "Don't get too full of yourself." As I jog towards her car trying to look as cool as possible, I could see her looking into her rearview mirror, trying to see if she looked good from all angles.

What she really didn't know is she didn't have to. She still had the natural beauty of a Goddess. Her body hadn't changed a bit over the past couple of years — in fact, from all the excess fucking I heard she was doing, she actually looked a lot thicker than before. She could see the arrogant look on my face as I jogged past the front window. I opened the door and hopped into the car, and she says, "I see you think because you put on a little weight and got some muscles, you think you're cute, huh?" She says this, not looking at me at all.

This was her backhanded way of giving me a compliment without really acknowledging it. I understood the game, so I played along. This was the part when she played "bitter ex" before she calmed her nerves and broke the ice to tell me what she really wanted. So we start riding and she continues to hit me up with backhanded compliments and taking jabs at the neighborhood I grew up in, when finally I had enough.

I ask her, "Damn is this all you came here for? If, so, let me out the car now dammit! I see you, and I'm thinking damn, what is she doing in my neck of the woods? It was a pleasant surprise, but now that you got to bumpin' your gums, I wish I hadn't seen your ass! So tell me, what did you come here for?" Sabrina pulls the car over next to a nearby park and says, "I apologize! I didn't really know how to come at you. It's been so long since I've seen or heard from you I didn't really know what to say.

"I mean, I heard you got this new girlfriend and you two have been together for some time now, and one of my girlfriends even told me you guys were going to get married. When I heard that, I knew I had to hurry back and come see you. Do you ever miss me at all, Willie?

"I mean did you ever wonder what was up with me or anything?" I tell her, "Of course I thought about you, but the one thing that stays on my mind most is when I saw you in the arms of another man. I cried for weeks after that. I stayed alone in my room where no one could see or hear me. That shit shook my foundation of what I thought love was, but now as I look back, and I see it was a situation I had to go through to make me a stronger man." Sabrina replies, "Dang, you went through all of that because of me?" I reply, "Yes I did. Don't get it twisted though, I went through that and fully recovered. Now I have no feelings where you are involved. I don't mean that in a bad way or with any malice intended, but I just know I went through those feelings and now I've moved on."

Sabrina sits back and looks into the distance and says, "You know Willie, I went to college with the expectations of becoming this well—

known, popular person that all the females liked and all the guys wanted to date, and I wound up doing that but in the process I started to hate what I became. My first two years in college you would've sworn I had lost my dag-gon mind. I slept with the popular guys on campus and hung out with the fast females, only realizing when I got to my junior year and saw the new booty freshmen doing the same things I did, how stupid I had to look. Now I know why the upper-class men would just look at me and shake their heads and talk shit about me. At the time, I just thought they were haters, and sure enough, some of them probably were, but for the most part they looked at me like that because they had been there before. After a lot of drunken binges and other stupid things my friends would always get mad at me, because all I would wind up talking about was you.

"'My Willie Woodson, or Willieworld,' as you like to be called. They would always tell me to shut up or go back and get with you if you meant that much to me, but I never did." Then I asked her, "Why did you always talk about me? When we were together I knew you loved me, but you never put too much on it. I mean, I never felt you were head over heels in love with me, because you stayed so focused on other things." She replies, "Willie. I finally came to realize those other guys only wanted to be with me because of how I looked. They were attracted to the nice body and the pretty face."

I interrupt and say, "Well it's nice to see you're still modest." Sabrina cuts me off and says, "Boy you know what I mean." We both share a slight chuckle and she continues, "What I'm trying to say is they never got past my physical attributes. That's all they were interested in. You were the only guy I knew who wanted me solely for me and I had to see you again to let you know that." I say, "So, you had to pop up here in the middle of the night to tell me that?"

She says "No, I was out having a drink with a girlfriend of mine and she encouraged me to muster up the strength and come see you. I figured you would be at Shea's house, so I went by there and he told me you had just left, so here I am. This wasn't a planned visit at all." "Damn, I'm impressed," I say. She says, "Willie, I just wanted you to know that you are my soulmate, and no matter what happens with you or me, I needed to tell you that so I could get it out of my system. Now that I've said it I can go on with my life."

At this time I didn't know what to think. I didn't know if she wanted me to be like, "Oh, that's all I wanted to hear. I think you're my soulmate too, now let's ride off into the beautiful sunset together," or what. The truth is, I always knew she was my soulmate too. There was never anyone who made me feel like this girl inside, but at the same time I had Belize now. Although I could never love Belize in the same way I did Sabrina, I knew Belize and I shared a strong love that was honest in a strange sense of the word.

With Sabrina, we would be the high-society, handsome man/beautiful woman ideal couple. The corporate world would be our oyster, but I wouldn't be close to being the man I wanted to be. I would always have to perform to her parents' standards, eat at the finest restaurants and be an all-around stuffy cat. With Belize I could be me at all times. If I wanted to smoke a little weed, it was my prerogative. I could wear what I wanted and swear when I got the urge. She never complained about it at all.

She let Willie be Willie. It was weird sometimes, because I thought if Belize were a little more like Sabrina or if Sabrina was a little more like Belize, I would have the perfect woman, but that's the same with everything. If this were a little more like that, this would be a perfect world. As it turns out, all Sabrina wanted to do was get that off her chest. She didn't expect anything to come out of our conversation. She says, "I know you have to be a little spooked at what I said but don't trip. I just came to you to see if you felt anything like I felt and to get all of that off my chest."

I replied, "Sabrina. "I've always felt you were my soulmate and always will. I know now, that I can never feel how I felt about you years ago, but I do know you are probably the only female I will be able to see as my soulmate." As I was talking, I could see tears welling in the eyes of Sabrina.

Looking at the tears well up in her eyes made a couple trickle down my cheeks. I was thinking to myself, "Damn, all I wanted to do was go home and get some sleep, and now I'm sitting here with my ex-chick, sobbing like a little girl. What the hell is going on?" I go on to tell her how I was so in love with her that the stress of seeing her with another dude made me lose my mind for a minute, and it took me a long time to get over those emotions. I went on to explain how I probably really never got over her, but Belize really helped me in dealing with it.

Sabrina and I laughed and talked until the sun came up. There was very little sexual tension between us two. We didn't really even think about going there. We watched the sun rise together and then she took me to the house. As I got out of the car, she also got out. She came around to the passenger side and gave me the biggest, deepest, most passionate hug she has ever given me. That was followed by a big fat kiss. She said, "Goodbye Willie. All of my numbers are the same and if you should ever need anyone to talk to about anything, be sure to give me a call. I love you." I told her I loved her too, and if she needed to call me she could call me at anytime also. And that was that. I watched her drive away and I went into the house to sleep the day away.

Although I knew we would never be together again, it made me think twice about my current relationship. It didn't make me think about leaving Belize or anything like that, but it did have me thinking about "what if". What if Sabrina and I were still together? What road would life be taking us down? The urge really wasn't strong enough for me to do anything about it, so that thought soon faded.

I slept the day away and got bombarded with questions as I woke up. First my mom lit into me. As soon as I woke up and went to the bathroom she said, "Boy, what the hell is wrong with you?" I replied, "What?" She says, "Boy, you just graduated from college and things are looking up for you, and now you want to stay out all night on drunken binges without calling me to let me know you're okay. What is going on, William Woodson?" I reply "Mom, why are you trippin'?" She says, "Trippin'? Trippin'? You ain't seen trippin yet. Wait until I tell your dad about what the hell is going on with his son. Then we'll see who's trippin'." At this point I'm thinking, "Damn, what the hell has gotten into this woman?"

I tell her "Moms, I apologize for not calling, but on my way home last night, I saw Sabrina and we talked until the sun came up." My moms says, "Sabrina? What the hell was she doing on this side of town? Well, never mind that. I apologize too, Willie. I realize you're grown now and you're a responsible adult, but I was just worried about you last night. You'll always be my baby, so I worry about you." As she says this, she walks over and gives me a hug, and starts to kiss me all over my cheeks and teasing me with her baby talk, saying, "My boobie, woobie, woobie, woo." I say, "Mom!" and playfully push her away, so I could go into my room and do my push-ups and sit-ups.

Before I could hit my first push-up, the phone rings. It's my boy Shea. The first thing he says is, "So, tell me what happened, nigga." I was like, "Tell you what happened with what?" He says, "Don't even try to play me like a fool, boy! I want to know what happened with you and Sabrina. Should I be expecting a crazy night out of you, like the one that happened with me?" I quickly said, "Ah, hell naw, nigga! Are you crazy? There's no way I'm about to be going through that shit. Anyway, nothing happened between Sabrina and I last night." Shea says, "Nigga, I know you're lying! I saw what she looked like last night, boy. She was looking good as hell and she was stalking you on the late night. There's no way you could convince me you didn't hit' em, man." I tell Shea, "Look, man. There's more to me and that girl than looks and sex. My love for her was deeper than that, so we just talked about things we needed to clear the air on and moved on. There was no sexual tension in the air and that's that." There was a short silence. I could tell Shea felt embarrassed, because he could feel the sincerity in my voice and he knew I was serious. After the short silence he clears the air and says, "Well I'll be damned. I thought that girl could still work her magic and have you dancing like a puppet, but I guess not."

I say, "Nigga, please! When have you known me to dance like a puppet for any breezy?" Shea says, "Anyway. Have you heard from your boy D-Luv?" I tell him, "No. I really don't expect to be hearing from that cat for a while. He seemed pretty spooked the last time we talked."

I asked him, "Have you heard from T?" Shea says, "No I think he's at the combines, trying to improve his draft stock." I say, "Oh yeah. I think he is out there." We continue to have our small talk about what's going on in our lives, like what jobs are hot, who's doing what in the street and what's going on with our girls. Then Shea burst out, "Oh yeah, I knew there was something I wanted to holla at you about. Man, one of these niggas told me one of the blood samples found in the park was HIV-positive." I was like, "What? Where did the nigga say he heard that?" Shea says, "Man, you know how that shit is, nobody knows exactly who said what. They heard it from somebody who heard it from somebody and all that shit." I was like, "Damn, here we go with that shit again." Shea says, "Willie, let me tell you something. Usually where there's smoke there's fire. By that I mean if this shit keeps popping up about D and HIV, there just might be some kind of truth to the shit. After all, the breezy Terry did page the nigga and told him to get tested, didn't she?" I replied, "Look here, man. You're getting just as bad as those niggas in the streets. I don't know and haven't heard of one heterosexual person coming down with that shit. Are you trying to tell me D is gay or something?" Shea says, "Naw man. I'm just saying, people are talking and the circle is closing in. You know I pray to God that nigga ain't got that shit, but fuck man, all fingers are pointing at our boy." I tell Shea, "Until we know for sure we should be on our boy's side and not buy in to what the streets are talking." Shea says,

"You're right, man. I'm going to keep an open mind and let things play out, but I'm definitely riding with D." After that, I told Shea I was going to hit my push-ups and sit-ups and then be on my way over to his house. He told me he was gonna be there all night, so it was cool to come through, and I told him I would be by there with a forty-ounce in hand for him.

I finally go to do my push-ups and sit-ups and hit the shower. I got dressed and told mom I was headed over to Shea's house. She says, "Don't have me worried all night." I tell her, "I won't, mom. If I come in too late I'll call you and let you know." She says, "O.K., I love you." I tell her, "I love you, too." And with that, I was down the stairs.

When I went to open the door, I had a big surprise as it opened. Belize was standing there. Opening the door and seeing her right there startled me, so I jumped back a little and she was like, "Damn, are you that shocked to see your woman, or were you expecting someone else?" I say, "Girl! You know damn well I wasn't expecting anyone else. I was just surprised to see anyone at my doorstep as soon as I opened my door." She then asks me, "Where are you going?"

I tell her, "I was on my way to Shea's crib." She says, "Wrong answer. You mean you were on your way to your woman's house." As she says this, she folds her arms. I say "Yeah, Yeah, that's it. I was on my way to my beautiful woman's house." She says, "Shouldn't you go back in the house and get some clothes?" I say, "Yeah, that's right.

Come on in and have a seat." She comes in the house and yells up the stairs, "Hello, Mrs. Woodson." My mom yells back down the stairs, "Hello! Who is that?" Belize says, "It's me, Belize." As she says this, she looks at me like, "Nigga, who the hell else you bring over here to meet your momma?" I run up the stairs and tell my mom, "I'm getting some clothes because I'm spending the night at Belize's house." My moms tell me, "Be careful and don't do anything I wouldn't do." I say, "Ha, ha, real funny mom. I'll see you tomorrow." I go downstairs and tell Belize, "Let's go." She gets up off the couch and says, "Bye, Mrs. Woodson!" My mom says, "Goodbye. You kids be good." Belize says, "We will!" Then she whispers in my ear, "Yeah, I'm gonna be real good to your baby boy, Mrs. Woodson." Just as we are exiting the door, my mom yells down the stairs, "I heard that!" Belize looked like she was turning into a dark red tomato. I just started laughing as loud as I could. Belize hit me on the shoulder and said, "Willie, that's not funny. Now your mom probably thinks I'm a tramp." I say, "She knows you're a tramp if you fuck with me." Belize gives me a glaring stare and I quickly say, "Damn. I'm just kidding!"

It was a short twenty-minute ride to Belize's house. Before we got to her house, she knew the routine. We stopped at the local mom and pop store so I could grab me a forty. I run in and out of the store, and off to her house we go. We get to Belize's house and as we enter, I could smell the incense burning. I turn to her and say, "Oh you came to my house with a plan, huh? You got the house all clean and smelling good and damn, is that chicken I smell coming from the kitchen?" She looks at me and says, "Don't worry about all that, just take your coat off and go over to the couch and watch television. I'm going to handle everything else." I say to her, "Alright then. Do what you do." I go over to the couch and flick on the tube. Draft day was coming up soon, so they were talking about how the talent was so deep this year and leading the pack was none other than my boy T.

All the analysts were saying he would be the first player taken, because the last place team drafted a quarterback the year before and they were looking to draft a running back this year. I was too excited for my boy, I yelled to Belize in the kitchen, "They're talking about my boy T again!" She yells back, "What are they saying?" Then I yell, "They're talking about how he's going to be the first player taken in the draft this year!"

She yells back, "Oh, that's cool!" I could tell she wasn't too much interested in my excitement for my boy, which really didn't bother me. Belize was not really an excitable person. The most excitement she ever displays is during sex, which I didn't mind at all either. About an hour went by. I could smell all of the aromas coming from the kitchen. I don't know what got into this woman or if someone told her I saw Sabrina or what but she hooked up a fat ghetto fabulous dinner, which consisted of fried chicken, mustard greens, mashed potatoes and gravy, and hot water cornbread.

I was like, "Whoa!" I asked Belize, "What did I do to deserve this?" She fires back, "Why can't I just be cooking a nice meal for my man? You haven't been out being a bad boy, have you? I know sometimes when people mess up and they get rewarded they feel guilty. Could that be you?" I reply, "First and foremost, hell no! I haven't been doing anything I should feel guilty about and secondly, you don't cook like this everyday, so I just thought I would ask. Now, with that being said, can I eat some of this good food you've labored so hard cooking for

me?" As I say this, I walk over and hug her from behind and kiss her gently on her neck.

She says, "Yes. Now go sit down at the table so I can fix your plate. I could see her smiling from ear to ear, even from behind. I sit down at the table and she fixes two plates, then we both dig in. I was somewhat surprised at how good the meal was. I knew she could cook up the more exotic foods, but she got down with the chicken, too.

This girl was collecting continuous bonus points with me. I don't know if it was woman's intuition or if this girl knows someone real close to me who's been talking, but she seems to always rise to the occasion. I guess that's why I've fallen in love with her over the years. After we eat and Belize washes all the dishes, we kick back and watch a couple of movies on television. We talk about everything from my boys

T, D-Luv and Shea to Belize's workplace having openings and world events. I like to talk to Belize because she always has interesting conversation.

Talking to her was like talking to one of the boys. I could open up to her and tell her things that I usually closely guard. She understood when I told her about my parents or when I told her how I felt about the D-Luv situation or anything in general. She never responded in a way that made me think, "Damn, that's the last time I tell her anything." She was very understanding that way. Actually, that's probably what really made her beautiful to me. I told her I would fill out an application at her job and see what would come of it. I wasn't too keen on getting a job with my girlfriend, but when it was all said and done, I would have a paycheck every two weeks and all it would be for me is a stepping-stone to another job and, more importantly, a bigger paycheck.

After the food settles in my stomach I start to give Belize the look. She looks at me and says, "Why are you looking at me like that," in a childish manner. I tell her, "You know why I'm looking at you like that." She starts to giggle and run around the room from me, but not too fast, because she really wants to get caught. Then I catch up to her and tackle her to the bed. In the midst of all of our heavy petting and fondling one another I hear the opening story on the news. It said, "Positive ID made to surviving suspect of murder mystery." I immediately stop kissing Belize and tell her to stop. She says, "What's the matter? What did I do?" I tell her, "Nothing. I want to see what the news is talking about." The news comes back on. It was the lead story. The news broadcaster says, "A positive ID has been given to the surviving suspect to this twisting murder mystery. He has been identified as Darrell Ray, a twenty-three year old black male who has also tested positive for HIV. If you see him, do not try to apprehend the suspect. He is considered to be armed and dangerous."

I turned the television off and sat in the darkness. My heart was somewhere buried deep in my body, beating a million miles a minute. I closed my eyes and put my hands over my face, and began to cry like a little teenaged girl who got her heart crushed for the first time. Belize came from behind and put her arms around me. She whispered in my ear, "Baby it's O.K. It's O.K., baby." As she rubbed my head and kissed me softly on my ear. I looked at her and I saw tears flowing down her cheeks also.

This only made us both cry more. We both hugged each other so tight we became one. Belize's phone starting ringing constantly; we knew it was either her friends or my boys trying to call and spread the ghetto gossip. Neither of us were in the mood to hear anyone, so Belize unplugged the phone and we cried ourselves to sleep.

Reaction

I woke up the next morning feeling like I had been ridden hard and put away. I was totally exhausted and emotionally drained. The alarm had been going off for about thirty minutes, and Belize hadn't moved one muscle. I called her name three or four times and the girl didn't even move. I pulled all of the covers off of her and she still didn't move an inch. Once I moved the blankets, her naked body was exposed and I still had my morning woody, so I started to kiss her buttocks.

I then got the right angle and slid my tongue around the coochie walls. It was amazing to me how I could call her name three or four times and the alarm could be blaring for thirty minutes and she was comatose, but as soon as I start licking the kitty—cat, her legs spread open instantly. She said to me in a raspy tone, "What are you doing?" I tell her, "Don't ask questions you already know the answer to. I know you learned that in college." She then says, "No. I was always taught to ask any question I wanted to know the answer to, even if I thought I knew the answer. Now shut up, and come up here and kiss me." I say, "No. You got that morning breath. I don't know if I want to fuck with you like that." She says, "You shouldn't talk. You now got coochie breath and I offered to kiss you." I tell her, "There's no better breath freshener in the morning, baby." She says, "I know that's right." I proceed to kiss my way from the cooch all the way to her lips.

From there, Belize grabbed hold of my penis and inserted it herself. I probably got in three or four pumps before she flipped me over and started riding like her name was the Lone Ranger. I felt like a two-dollar tramp. Her eyes were still closed and she was going to town on me. This girl had to cum twice within ten minutes of insertion. Meanwhile, my toes couldn't curl back any further, and I couldn't hold it back any longer. I told her, "I'm about to cum!" She says, "Come on, baby. Cum for momma." I said, "Here it comes, baby!"

With that, she started riding at the speed of light and I let out a roar so loud the neighbors probably thought a wild grizzly got loose in the neighborhood. Belize just collapses on top of me. She says, "Oh my God! I needed that!" I say, "Shit. If I hadn't initiated the action, I think I would have to call that date rape." She says, "Shut up" in a shy, somewhat embarrassed voice."

All the while, the alarm clock is still going off. I tell her, "You must not be going to work today, huh?" She says, "You know what? I haven't missed one day of work since I started and I've never been late. I think I deserve one day off, don't you think?" I say, "After what you just did and last night, I'd have to agree with that statement." Belize then plugs the phone back in and calls in sick to work. Her boss asked her a million questions because she never called in sick before.

He was asking was everything o.k. with her health, family and personal life. She kept reiterating that she just didn't feel good and she would be in the next day and there was no problem beyond that, but I guess he was really concerned because she was such a reliable person. When she hung the phone up, I was like, "Damn, did the nigga want a stool sample too? If I didn't trust you and didn't know he looked like Chewbacca, I would swear up and down that he hit the booty before." She then says, "Boy, be quiet. You know that old man is just concerned about me like I was his daughter." I then say, "Well you know down south, father and daughter relationships are very special."

She then gives me the death look and turns back over. The phone rings about five minutes later. Belize says, "Willie,can you get that? I'm too exhausted to move." I then say, "Shit. I'm exhausted too. Let that shit ring." Belize then climbs over me and answers the phone. She says, "Hello!" Then she tosses me the phone and says, "It's for you anyway." I say, "Hello?" It was Shea on the other end, and he says in a somber voice, "What's up, boy? What are you getting into today?" I tell him, "Belize took the day off and I think we're going to hang out for the rest of the day." He says, "Cynthia took the day off too, and, so did I. You guys want to hook up and do something?" I say "Yeah. Maybe we could go to lunch or catch a flick or something like that." He says, "That sounds cool to me." I say, "Is twelve o'clock cool for you guys?" Shea says, "Alright, then." Just as he was about to hang up he says, "Oh yeah. I almost forgot why I called you over there. I know you saw the news last night, boy." I say, "Yeah, man. I'm still exhausted from all the emotions I went through last night." Shea says, "Man. It's good to know I wasn't the only one. Cynthia had to come over and spend the night because I couldn't get in touch with you and T was still out of town and niggas was poppin' up over the house talking big shit. I thought I was going to go crazy over that shit, man." I told him, "Man, I was crying like a big bitch and couldn't control it. I felt like someone told me my best friend had died." Shea then says, "Well, in essence, that's what happened, wasn't it? Once you get that shit life, as you know, it is over." I then say to Shea, "I don't know, man. I think he might be cool for a minute with that HIV shit, but if you have full-blown AIDS, that's when you can start making funeral arrangements." Shea then says "What's the difference, man? Isn't it more like with HIV, you only have a year or two before it becomes full-blown A.I.D.S. anyway? So, anyway you look at it, our boy is a walking time bomb."

"What would you do if you seen him and he tried to shake your hand or asked to share a beer you were drinking?" I say, "I don't know. In any case, let me get this girl up, so we could get in motion." Shea then says, "Alright, then. So we should expect to see you guys at the house around twelvish?" I then say, "We'll be there, man." We both hang up and Belize curls under me and says, "What you got us doing today, baby?" I then tell her, "Shea and Cynthia both took the day off also, so we're going to meet them for lunch." She then says, "That sounds good, but I need to go back to sleep. I'm exhausted."

I was like, "Well I need to flip this television on so I could watch the draft and see where my boy goes." I turn on the tube and the draft is just getting started. The first thing they do is highlight the big blue-eyed stud quarterback. His story was actually intriguing. I just figured he was one of those silver-spoon white boys who had it good from birth, but it was quite the contrary. As it turned out, he lost both his mom and dad at a young age. His mom actually died giving birth to him and his dad was killed on a construction site.

He wound up going to live with his aunt and uncle who live not too far from a Los Angeles project housing unit, and he grew up learning to play football with the brothers from the projects. He gave a lot of credit for his success to the people he grew up playing football in the streets with. He even had his little walk on the wild side. He got in some trouble with his neighborhood friends and had to spend a night in jail.

He called his aunt and uncle to bail him out and they declined. His aunt and uncle wanted to teach him a lesson and let him know that this is what happens when you choose to do bad things. He said that night was when he decided it was only going to be football and school for him. No more trying to live the fast life. He even got one of his childhood friends a scholarship to the school he went to.

By the time they finished profiling him, I became a fan. It goes to show you, you can never judge a book by its cover. After they profile him, I expect them to profile my boy T, but they go right to the first choice. Now since they only profiled one player and they were about to pick, I just knew my boy wasn't going to be the first pick. The television does a split screen between my boy T and blonde, blue eyes before they announce the first pick. I got my fingers crossed for my boy and they then announce, "With the first pick in the draft, the Dallas Cowboys select Terrance Bronson." My boy T is elated. They show him turn to his mom and give her a hug, then he turns to his girl and gives her a hug before he goes to the podium. I start jumping like a madman in the bed. Belize turns to me and says, "Willie, what the hell is wrong with you, boy? You see I'm trying to get some sleep." I just turn to her and say, "My boy was just the number one draft pick! I'm happy as hell baby!" I then jump on top of her and give her a big kiss. She says, "O.K., O.K., I'm happy for your boy too, now can you please stop jumping around, I'm getting a headache." I say, "I apologize, baby. I'm just ecstatic for my boy and I had to let it show." After I said that, it was like I remembered how tired I was. After all, in a twelve-hour period I went from being the saddest I had ever been in my life after hearing about my boy D-Luv, to being close to the happiest I had ever been after seeing my boy T being drafted and got date-raped in-between. All of a sudden, the emotional roller coaster took its toll and I was back to sleep again.

The next thing I know, Belize is showered, fully dressed and jumping up and down on the bed yelling, "Wake up sleepy head! Its eleven o'clock. Wake that ass up, sir!" I jump up, tackle her, and say, "I am up, dammit!" I was still in a drowsy state, but I couldn't let her think she was getting the best of me. So I tried to play it off like her jumping on the bed didn't bother me. I gt showered up and we're on our way to Shea's house.

On the way over there, things were kind of quiet in the car. Belize asks, "Is everything okay?" I reply, "Yeah. Why do you ask that?" She says, "Well it's been a fairly tumultuous night and morning, so I just wanted to make sure my boo-boo was okay. You've been to both extremes in a short period of time, you know." I reply, "Thanks for the concern babe, but I'm cool, and I want to thank you for being there for me."

"You don't know how good this makes me feel." She then says, "Since you're being so introspective right now, I want to let you in on a little secret." I say, "Oh shit. Is this going to ruin my morning? You know I'm somewhat unstable right now." She says, "No, but I wasn't completely honest with you yesterday." I then say, "What?" She says, "Well, the reason I cooked for you yesterday was because you did do something good." Still not knowing what the hell she was talking about, I ask again, "What?" "She says, "Well, first you have to promise that you won't be mad." I say, "Girl if you don't tell me what the hell you need to tell me, I'm about to get mad as hell." She stops me from rambling and says, "Well I talked to Cynthia yesterday and she talked to Shea and he told her that you really must love me." I stop her and say, "Well, you should know that already." She says, "Wait. I'm not done. He told her you saw Sabrina on the late night when you were walking home and you talked to her until the sun came up and didn't do the nasty with her. Now when I first heard this, I must admit, I was pretty upset. Then I went from being upset to being hurt. Then I realized that she was part of your past and you guys did share love, but the thing that really impressed me was the fact that you kept your pants on. Most guys would've had sex with the girl even if they didn't love them anymore. You really just proved to me what I already knew!" I then asked, "And what is that?" She grabbed my hand and kissed it, saying, "You are a special man and that's why I love you."

Before I try to tell her I love her too, she interrupts me and says, "Oh before I forget. Don't say anything to Shea. I promised Cynthia I wouldn't say anything and if she found out you knew she would hate me and then her and Shea would be going at it. So promise me Willie Woodson." I then say, "Yeah, yeah, I promise. You know what though?" She asks, "What?" I then tell her, "I'm not mad at him. I would like to think he meant well by divulging that information to Cynthia anyway. And I know Cynthia told you to let you know how much you mean to me, so it's all good." Belize then says, "Yeah, you're probably right. Which is all the more reason not to say anything, okay babe?" I then say, "Look. I'm not going to say anything, alright? Now let's just hook up with Shea and Cynthia and eat. I could eat the backend of a damn Wombat, I'm so hungry." Belize laughs and shakes her head as usual from my crazy jokes, and we pull up at Shea's. Shea and Cynthia are already coming out of the door when we arrive. Shea says, "Damn. It's about time ya'll got her. I was just about to pour some chocolate on Cynthia's arms and start to eat her if ya'll took any longer." Cynthia then says, "Sorry dear, that was last night you're thinking about." She and Belize then look at each other with devilish grins. We all pile into Belize's car and head out to eat.

The whole ride over there was spent on the topic of last night's news. Shea was saying how he thought we would never hear from D-Luv again because he would be too ashamed to show his face again. The girls seemed to think that he would somehow get in touch with one of us soon. I tended to side with the girls. My reason was that D-Luv didn't really communicate with family anymore, and other than them, we were the only family he had. More specifically, I felt he would be in touch with me because he knew I had love for him like a brother, and I would lend him a helping hand, no matter what the circumstance.

We get to the restaurant and order like we never ate before. Shea and I ordered the biscuits and gravy while the women order French toast. All of us must've ordered one of each side order they had on the menu and there was complete silence once the food came. Cynthia and Belize scarfed down their food faster then Shea and I. I looked at Shea and said, "Hey this might be a day we want to remember. Both of our girls are eating more than us men. "

Shea and I look at each other and I say, "One of these days that weight is gonna stay put instead of the body breaking it down and burning if off. You ladies do know your metabolism slows down when you get older, right?" They both look at me, then they look at each other, then simultaneously, they flip me off. Belize then says, "Nigga, do you think I wasn't feeding you all of that fattening home-cooked food without a purpose last night? I guarantee you that you will put on a lot more weight, a lot faster than I ever will. I don't do push-ups and sit-ups every morning and I still manage to keep my shape, thank you. I mean, you're always going to be my baby, but when those other chicks see that belly, they're gonna run from you." She then looks at Cynthia and gives her a high five. I then say, "Yeah, that plan sounds real good, but luckily for me I'll be calling an audible on that one and I'll continue to be in shape and look good. Now. Thank you."

We shot the breeze for about another twenty or thirty minutes, then the ladies excused themselves to go to the bathroom. Shea and I sat at the table and he turns to me and says, "O.K., playa, it's time for some of that real talk shit. Now that I got you here face to face you can tell me. Did you or did you not tap Sabrina's drawls that night?" I look him dead in the eyes and say, "No. I told you, I didn't even think about tapping man. It's not only because I'm in love with Belize, it's also because a nigga's just changing, man. Ever since those rumors about D-Luv popped up way back in the day I started to change my sexual habits. Now that I know the nigga got that shit and I know he's not a rump ranger, I'm extra careful with my decision making on whom I will and will not sleep with." Shea looks at me with that deer-in-the-headlights look and says, "Yeah I guess you're right, man. I've been working so hard and kickin' it with the fellas at the house so much, I haven't really tripped about my sexual activities on the side coming to a complete halt. When I really think about it, I think I stopped fucking around, around the time all the rumors about D-Luv started, too. I guess it's some kind of subconscious shit, man." I say, "Maybe it is. At any rate, I ain't trying to catch that shit, man. Right now our boy probably feels like the town leper. He ain't trying to be seen by nobody." Shea then says, "I know you watched that draft, man! T fucked around and got drafted number one. Do you know what that means, man? That boy is gonna have more breezy jocking him than you can shake a stick at." I then say, "Yeah, our boy's gonna have it bad from all angles for a minute. Trifling hoes, money-hungry friends and relatives. But hey, the bad comes with the good. I think if we stay true to our boy and help him weed out some of those leeches, he'll be alright."

Just then, the girls come back. Shea says "Damn, was ya'll shittin' in stalls right next to each other, choppin' it up or something?" Cynthia says, "Fuck you!" I just laugh as we get up to exit out of the restaurant. My boy Shea is good for saying what's on his mind, and I love him for that.

On the way back to Shea's, I tell Belize to drop me off at his house and I would just walk home. Belize gives me a look like, "What the hell part of the plan is this?", and she begrudgingly says, "O.K., but I have to talk to you for a minute before you get out of the car." I just shake my head up and down because I know what's coming next. I look in the rearview mirror and I can see Shea laughing, because he also knows what I'm in for.

As we pull up to Shea's house, Cynthia taps Belize on the shoulder and says, "Girl, when you're about to leave, honk your horn so I can catch a ride with you." Belize says, "O.K., girl. You know that's not a problem." Then she turns to me and says, "What's up, Willie? I thought we would spend the rest of the day together, since I took off work to be with you. What's really going on, baby?" I look her straight in the eyes and say, "Look babe. I appreciate you taking the day off work and being there for me in my time of need, but I really need to holla at Shea. We both just found out our potna got that shit and it's devastating news to the both of us. We're going to have to deal with niggas coming up to us talking shit about our potna, spreading rumors about him being gay, and all types of shit. We have to huddle and see how we're going to approach these situations, and better yet we have to talk to each other and see how we feel and how we're dealing with this." Belize, forever my understanding friend and lover, looks at me, rubs her gentle hand down my check, kisses me and says, "I'm sorry, baby. I know I'm being selfish right now and you need to holla your boy, but you know I'm only this way because I love you, right? I was only thinking of what I wanted. I understand what you need to do, so go handle that and maybe I can see you later." I say "Baby, you will definitely see me later. I'll call you when I'm done here and then I'll have Shea take me to the house and get some clothes and then drop me off at your house." She excitedly says, "You know you don't have to call. I'm just going to drop Cynthia off and go home. Even if I do wind up kickin' it with her for a minute, it won't be as long as you guys are gonna be together, so I'll be home. Just come on by. No calls needed."

I then give her a kiss and say, "I love you, Belize." Her eyes lit up like Christmas trees. She says, "You know, you're the first guy to ever say that to me, and I actually felt you meant it. I have friends who tell me their boyfriends tell them they love them and they catch the nigga with the next broad, but I know you Willie. You don't say things you don't mean, and that's why I've never forced the issue. I knew someday it would come. I love you too, babe! Now go on and talk to your boy, so I can gloat to Cynthia."

She plants a big kiss on me and honks the horn as I exit. As I look at her when I walk away, I could see a big smile on her face from cheek to cheek. I didn't know that telling her I loved her would make her feel that way. I always assumed that she just knew without me saying anything to her. As I turn to walk towards Shea's house Cynthia comes walking past and says "Alright Willie, I'll see you later. While you're over here chillin' with your friend, can you please teach him some manners?" With that, she hops into the car with Belize and they drive off. As I open the door, Shea is pulling his pants up and buttoning them. I say, "What the hell was going on in here?"

Shea says, "Man, I had to get me a quick one before she left, and I knew I had until the car horn went off to get me one." I said, "God damn. I think you might have broken the world record for quickies, boy." Shea says, "Brah. I was hoping Belize would have you hemmed up for a second, because she looked like she meant serious business when she said she wanted to talk to you. I then say, "She did have me hemmed up for a second, and I do mean a second. That's why I say I think you have the new world record for quickies."

Shea then says, "Whatever, nigga. You want to walk to the store to get something to drink?" I say, "You know it, boy." It was a nice day outside, so there were a lot of people out and about enjoying the California sun. No sooner than five minutes into our walk, we see Sandals making his way towards us, and bringing up the rear with him was White Shit. Shea just looked at me and said, "Are you ready, boy?"

I look at him and say, "Fuck it. Better sooner than later, and better yet, we get to start off with amateurs." Just then, Sandals comes up with a little smirk on his face and says, "What's up with your boy, man? That nigga is killing motherfuckers and got that shit. Man, that nigga is off the hook. I heard he might have been swinging both ways and shit, man. What's up with that?" I look at Shea and say, "Man, I told you bitch niggas was gonna be talking like hoes and spreadin' that punk shit." Shea looked at me with an expression on his face that read, "My nigga, I was hoping we were gonna take that route with this shit." Then Shea chimed in, saying, "Yeah, man. Niggas that don't know what they talking 'bout need to shut the fuck up and not even speak on grown folks' business."

Neither one of us even looked at Sandals when we were speaking, but we could tell he started to feel like a turtle who stuck his head out a little too soon and slowly slid his slimy head back into his shell. Forever the hard headed one, White Shit noticed Sandals reeling, and said, "Ah niggas, ya'll can't get mad. The streets are talking and your boy's name is ringin' off the hook. What my retarded compadre was trying to convey was niggas is talking about that shit out here. To add on to that, every nigga is stressing over what hoes they done ran up in over the last five years."

"Everybody knows that D-Luv damn near fucked everything movin'. Shit, before I even started talking about this shit, I had to make sure I didn't share any common hoes with the nigga. To tell the truth, I still really don't know, so if any of ya'll niggas shared a drink with me, you better beware." After White Shit's statement, Shea and I couldn't do anything but look at each other and shake our heads simultaneously. After Sandals eases his head out of his shell, he asks us where we were going. We told him and White Shit we were on our way to the store and then they joined us. They were running down all of the rumors people were spreading in the town. I couldn't believe some of the shit I was hearing. There was one rumor that was super outlandish.

Some people actually believed that D-Luv made a deal with the cats he, Nino and Vell were selling the dope to and killed his cousin and Nino. Then, he supposedly double-crossed the other cats and killed them too when he realized what he had done. I honestly couldn't believe people could be so stupid and gullible. Oh well, that goes to show you how things could get when people are misinformed and start speculating.

We made our way to the store and Shea and I each bought a fifth of Sapphire Gin and a gallon of orange juice. When we were making our purchase, I looked at Shea and he gave me the look. The look he gave me suggested he knew exactly what I was thinking. He confirmed it when he said, "I know, nigga. I'm not going to drink that much." We still get both bottles but only one of them was gonna be opened on this night. Shea looks at me and says, "As a matter of fact you could take that motherfucker when you leave tonight. I look at him and say, "Oh, I already planned on taking this bitch with me when I leave the party."

Sandals and White Shit look at each other and start laughing. Shea looks at them and says, "I don't know why ya'll niggas is laughing. Ya'll gon' be lucky if you even get to taste this shit." White Shit looks at Shea and says, "Ah nigga let me know if I can't drink right now and I'll get my own shit." Shea says, "Shut up nigga and grab another gallon of orange juice." White Shit gets the orange juice and we make our way back to Shea's house. When we get back to Shea's house, everybody fixes their own drink and we settle in. It just so happens the news is on, once everyone has their drinks and sits down. The first story they lead into is about D-Luv. The news reporter says, "Once again, police say they have no leads on the whereabouts of Darrell Ray. He is the suspect in a gruesome homicide that left four men dead." After he says this they put a picture if D-Luv on the screen. He then continues, "If anyone has any knowledge of his whereabouts, please call the Oakland Police Deptartment and give them the information. Do not try to apprehend the suspect. He is considered to be armed and very dangerous."

White Shit then blurts out, "Damn! This nigga D-Luv is the star of a damn murder mystery slash horror film. This is some unreal shit. I know one of you niggas know where he is, man." He says this looking at Shea and me. I say, "Man, I haven't the slightest clue, and even if I did you know damn well I would say shit to your ass." Shea lifts his head out of his drink and says, "Ditto." Everyone gets quiet for a minute and we start watching a movie on television; then Sandals has to break the silence and says, "Man. What do you think is going through D-Luv's mind right now? I mean, I'm not saying this on some bullshit. I mean, he knows he's going to die. That's fact number one. Then he also knows when the police catch his ass he's going to jail, so no matter what, he's fucked. He's going to die slowly on the run or he's going to die slowly in jail. There ain't no way he could get out of either one of those terrible endings. On top of that, I hear that some of these bitches he fucked, their brothers, uncles and cousins want to kill the nigga." I wasn't used to Sandals saying anything that made so much sense, so I had to gather my thoughts real quick but what he said made a lot of sense. D-Luv had to be a mess. He knew his ending in this life was going to be a sad one. No matter how hard-core you are in the face of death, death is going to win when it decides it's your time to go.

Time starts to fly by and pretty soon Sandals and White Shit decide to leave. Shea and I sit up and talk a little longer then the doorbell rings. Shea opens the door and says, "It's for you, Willie." Since I had a bad angle and couldn't see who was at the door, Shea kept his same tired facial expression when he answered the door, so I knew it couldn't be too much of a surprise. Then Belize walks through the door. She says, "You know you're not going home tonight, right? I already went by your house and talked to your mom and got you some clothes, so come on with momma." The first thing that went through my head was, "Damn this girl is lucky I love her because if any other broad I messed with did the same thing, I'd certify them as being erased, but since Belize had the all-good pass, I appreciated what she did." I told Shea, "I guess you'll know where to find me, huh, nigga." He says, "I guess so." Belize then says, "Oh, Cynthia is on her way over here too, Shea." Shea looks at me and says, "Boy we might have started some shit getting those two girls together." I give Shea a pound and start to walk out the door.

As I'm walking out of door, the phone rings. Shea goes to answer it and as I'm leaving he says, "Willie, telephone." I walk to the phone and ask, "Who is it, my mom?" Shea says, "No. It's D-Luv, nigga!" I get on the phone and say, "Hello." D-Luv then says, "What's up Willie?", in a mundane sort of tone. I'm kind of nervous and caught off guard at this juncture, and I ask him, "What's up?" He says, "Nothing, everything, and all kinds of other shit. I'm not calling to keep you up over Shea's or anything. I knew you would be at his house if you weren't at home. I just called to let you know I was gonna be back in town tomorrow, and I wanted to holla at you." I tell him, "You know it's all good. Just let me know when and where." He then tells me, "I'll call your mom's house tomorrow at about one o'clock. Is that cool?" I say "Yeah. I'll be there." Then we say our goodbyes and hang up. Shea asks, "What did he say, man?" I tell him, "He said he wants to holla at me tomorrow." Shea says, "Damn! You want me to come with you?" I tell him, "Naw. I should be cool. I'm a holla at you tomorrow man. I'll let you know what's up."

I then leave and go over to Belize's house. I had a weird feeling in the pit of my stomach, but sleeping in the arms of my girl that night made me feel a lot better. I couldn't wait to see what the next day would bring.

The night with Belize came and went in a blink of the eye. We had our usual deep conversation before our deep passionate romp in the sack and then comatose sleep. Belize had to go to work the next morning, and I told her to drop me off at the house on her way to work. She let me know I could've just slept at her house and went home when I wanted to, but I told her I had things to do and she wound up dropping me off at the house. I told her I would see her later. We kissed and she was off to work.

It was still about seven o'clock in the morning, so my moms was getting ready for work. As I came in, she said, "Who are you, young man? I mean, I remember I had a son but I don't get to see him much because he has another woman in his life now. Could you be him?" I say, "What's up mom? You know you're the only woman for me." My mom replies, "Um, hmm. I used to be. I'm just kidding with you, son. Belize is a very good woman and if you choose to be serious with her I can back that decision all the way." I tell my mom, "She's a very intelligent young lady and she's definitely the one right now, and I do know I love her and can see myself with her for a long time." My mom then says, "You young men kill me. I don't even think you understand what you just said, but anyway let me tell you this. There won't be too many people or should I say women you will meet in your life like Belize, so don't take her love for granted, thinking you could find something better. You got a beautiful, intelligent young lady who will do anything for your little stinky booty. So don't go looking when you don't need to." She then switches her demeanor and says, "Well that's enough preaching for me. If I don't get out of here, I'm going to be late for work, so I'll see you later, son. Or I think I will be seeing you later. Are you spending the night at Belize's?"

I reply, "Yes mom, probably so." She then says, "See, you do have another woman in your life. Anyway, have fun and call me to let me know you're safe." I tell my mom I'll call her and let her know what I'm doing later, and she's out the door. I go to my room and hit my push-ups and sit-ups for the day. I start to get on edge, thinking about seeing D-Luv. I didn't have a clue as to what I would say to him when I saw him. I kept having visions of him standing at my doorstep looking all skinny and having lesions and things. I didn't know what to think. The bottom line was, I had to be as normal as possible. Even if I was trying to be normal, I couldn't come off as being cruel, no matter how phony it looked. There were some weird thoughts going through my mind. After I showered up and got dressed, I went downstairs to watch some television. Before I knew it, I wound up taking a nap and the television was watching me.

The day slowly crept along and I could feel the sun creeping along my face through the window when the afternoon approached. Then I was awakened by the doorbell. I looked at the clock and it was one on the dot. I didn't even bother to ask who it was. I knew it would be D-Luv. I opened the door and said, "What's up." It was D-Luv standing there looking like his ballin' ass self. He was clean cut, freshly dressed and smelled like the best cologne. He said, "What's up Willieworld?", in a mellow monotone voice. I say, "Come in man." D-Luv comes in and we sit down with the television now on videos. I watched D-Luv's every move.

I was expecting to see something different in his character that would give me the signal that he had HIV, but there was none. He was exactly the same. I didn't have to wait long for my first test. D-Luv asked me for a cup of water. Normally I would just pick any cup, fill it with water and give it to him to drink. Now I'm looking for the least-used cup in the house that I could possibly dispose of, after he used it. I felt so weird in the pit of my stomach for doing this, but it was like I was really thinking of it. It seemed like the natural thing to do. I come back into the living room with D-Luv's water. He looked at me as I handed him his cup, he then looked at the cup. He said, "Damn, You guys actually use this to drink? It looks like it was meant for the dog, if you had one." I quickly respond, "Ah man, we need to wash dishes. It was one of the last clean cups." Luckily for me, I had a bunch of dirty dishes in the sink my moms wanted me to wash. D-Luv continues to drink his water.

We watch some videos in silence as he drinks his water, and then he says, "I bet you're wondering why I'm here, huh?" I say, "Well, I know you said I'm one of the few people you keep in contact with, so I was expecting to hear from you. On the other hand, I figured you would be calling from some remote location on the run." D-Luv said, "The thought had crossed my mind, but hell, how long can you run? Where could I really go and live normal, knowing what I know about myself? Nowhere, man. On the real Willie, I came back here to cleanse my soul." I said, "What do you mean 'cleanse your soul'?" D-Luv said, "Exactly what I said, man. I really don't want to put the burden on you, like you're some kind of preacher or something, but you're the most responsible person I know and the one I feel the most comfortable talking to." I say, "Really? What do you have to say that I don't know? To put it bluntly, I know you've killed and I know you have a deadly disease with no cure. That might seem a little cold and basic, but I don't think you would want to get into the details of a lot of things with me." D-Luv then says, "That's where you're wrong. There are a lot of things that are heavy on my soul right now, and I wanted to holla at someone I knew about them. I want someone to know the truth about Darrell Ray. I don't want people to go off on what the newspapers have to say, and definitely not what the rumor mill has to say." I then look him dead in his eyes and say, "Alright. Tell me what's on your mind." I then tell D-Luv to hold on while I poured us both a shot of Christian Brothers from the cupboard. D-Luv declined my offer for a drink, but I felt I was gonna need one.

I position myself comfortably back on the couch and D-Luv begins. He says, "Willie, do you remember when all of those rumors about me having HIV started?" I say, "Yes." He says "Man I probably had that shit way back then. Since that time I've always felt a little different and I knew my sexual behavior leading up to that point. Man, I fucked everything that moved from the most beautiful females to the most hideous. I don't know why because I didn't need to, but I just did.

"I knew Terry was a super freak and everybody hit, but I would still run up in her on the late night. I refused to use a rubber with every chick and the ironic thing about that is Terry was one of the few to ask me to use one. I did nasty things with that girl, man." I then inquisitively ask, "Like what?" He said, "We would do it when she was on her period man, and even one worse, I would fuck her in the ass with my bloody dick."

When this nigga said that, my whole body language changed. I started cringing in my seat. I just had this icky feeling like I had slime all over my body. I then had to ask him, "What in God's name made you want to do some shit like that?" He said, "I don't know man. She even said it was the sickest shit she ever did but she never bothered to stop me. We just did it over and over again. She was the only female I would do that type of sick shit with too man. I just felt like only gay dudes could get AIDS or HIV, so I never really tripped on my sexual-behavior until I started hearing about heterosexuals getting the disease. Even when I heard that, I always figured the people getting the disease were either closet homosexuals or bisexuals.

"These past couple of days I've been hiding out with Terry. She looks horrible, man. That shit is eating her up fast and I think it's only a matter of time for me too." I then say, "Man they're coming up with new advanced medicines every day. You never know how they can help unless you get some medical attention."

D-Luv looks at me and says, "Brah, you're acting like I ain't wanted for murder! My ass is between a rock and a hard place, man. Medical attention can't do shit for me now. The only thing left for me to do is decide how I'm going out. My story is already coming to a conclusion. It's all about whether I'm going out in a blaze or quietly into the night."

I said, "What do you mean by that, D? I know you ain't planning on doing something stupid." He then says, "What do you mean 'something stupid'? I've already been about as stupid as you can get. That's why I'm facing the circumstances I'm facing now. I can't possibly do anything any more stupid than I've already done." After he says this, my doorbell rings. I haven't a clue who this could be I look at D-Luv and say, "Go to the back. I'm not expecting company, so I don't know who the hell this might be." D-Luv gets up from the couch and scurries to the back of the house. I go to the door and ask, "Who is it?" On the other side of the door Shea says, "It's me! And I brought you a surprise." I slowly open the door and Shea is standing there with our boy T.

Excitedly, I rush over to my boy and give him a big hug and say, "Congratulations, Man. I told you all that jacking off would pay off for you someday!" He says, "Thank you and fuck you very much!" As they walk in the house, T says, "Man, I miss you boys so much, man. It's been like a wild circus lately. I haven't had any time to get all of my faculties together. I'm still reeling and don't know what the hell is going on yet." Shea then says, "Well that big ass Mercedes will bring your ass to reality real quick." I then say, "Oh you got that big body huh? What does your girl think about that?" T says, "Man, I don't even want to talk about that tramp right now." Shea and I look at each other and say, "O.K." Then a voice from the back of the house says, "Can I join in the celebration?" T and Shea say, "Who is that?" I say, "Let's go to the back and find out."

We walk to the back and the door to the back yard is open. We walk outside and D-Luv is standing with his back to us, looking at the train tracks across the way. He turns around and says, "What up Shea?" Shea nods his head and says, "What up Man?" D-Luv then says, "Congratulations, T. Everybody always knew you would be in the NFL someday." T says, "Thanks man." D-Luv looks at how Shea and T keep their distance and says, "My, has the time strained our friendship. I remember a time when you cats would jump at the chance to give me a pound or a hug. It's okay though. I understand the circumstances that causes your apprehension. Looking at all three of you guys together again, all grown up, makes me proud. Especially you, Shea. I heard you went to school and you've been working steadily, handling your business. That's real cool, man. I always wondered what route you were gonna take, because you didn't have much direction. I'm glad you took the right route. As for you, Willie, I think the world ain't ready for what you have to offer yet. You're the coolest thing on two legs, man. A true hood nigga at heart but you know you have to do that square thing to survive. You're a rare breed man, and I love that about you. Don't ever change, man."

He then turns and looks at T and says, "What can I say about you, boy. Ain't nothing like seeing the fruits of your labor. You actually did it and you did it, big man. I'm proud of you." I then look at D and say, "What is this, man? Is this your farewell or something? Are you turning yourself in? Going on the run? What?" D-Luv then says," I told you I couldn't live on the run, Willie. I'm for damn sure not going to jail, man. I just wanted to see you guys for the last time and let you now I feel.

After he makes that statement, he pulls out a nickel-plated nine millimeter. The sun hit it in a way that made us all cover our eyes from the reflection. We all recovered quickly enough to realize what this nigga was about to do. In unison we all said, "No, D! Don't do this, man! No, Man! Please, don't do it!" We all kept our distance because we didn't want to make any quick moves, but I tried to walk towards him slowly. But he said, "Willie, I know what you're trying to do, but don't. Just remember me when I was shining. When I was the hottest thing in the town. They can never take that away from me man, never."

With that, D-Luv put the gun to his head and "Boom!", he pulled trigger. His body hit the ground like a ton of bricks.

T, Shea and I stood in shock, shaking where we stood. I hit my knees and started crying uncontrollably. T and Shea both turned to separate walls in the back yard, hid their heads and started crying hysterically. D-Luv's body lay in a puddle of blood with smoke coming out of one side of his head. His chapter was now over. He went out in a blaze, but definitely not a blaze of glory. That day changed us forever.

Time passed rapidly after Darrell Ray killed himself. The funeral came and went. People were spreading rumors about my man as they lowered his body under the earth. I spoke good things about D-Luv at his funeral. I let people know he was a kind-hearted young man who just took the wrong route in life. I let people know he could've been anything he wanted to be, because he was intelligent enough to do so. I let people make their own choices from there. It changed T, Shea and I more than we would ever know.

I immediately settled down with Belize, permanently. I asked her to marry me, and she said yes. I bumped around for a minute and then found my niche counseling kids. Belize and I then had twin girls of our own.

I never cheated on her and never will. I feel my purpose is to be strong and D-Luv saw that in me — that's what I'll keep as his legacy. My love for Belize far outweighs the love I once felt for Sabrina. I can't imagine my life without her warmth and kindness. As it turns out, she was the perfect female for me. It also taught me a valuable lesson in life. At one time I remember I held this woman at tramp status, for the way that we met one another, but life took us on an amazing journey. God will teach you many lessons when you're least expecting to be taught.

Shea also got married. He and Cynthia tied the knot and had a little boy. Cynthia also became the District Manager of a Video Store chain. Shea stresses and complains as usual, but he's also responsible and takes care of his business. He and Cynthia are doing very good. Shea became a manager at a freight-forwarding company, and he's making good money and taking care of his family.

Terrance took the bachelor route. His so-called love decided she wanted to sleep with one of his college buddies and that changed T forever. The only ones he would ever trust was me and Shea. A couple of his college buddies took advantage of his friendship in ways T wouldn't divulge to us, and his girl took advantage of his love. Luckily for him, he found out about this before he was drafted. He planned on marrying her and having kids soon after being drafted, but she blew the thought of any of those dreams for T. T bounced back pretty quickly, though. He wound up being a very happy bachelor and he stayed, packing condoms so he wouldn't suffer the same fate as D-Luv. We all went through a lot during our ordeal. Each one of us handled D-Luv's death differently, but it made us all more responsible.

Sometimes I think God puts people in situations just to help others better themselves. By this, I mean maybe God put D-Luv in our lives specifically to let us know that we had to be more responsible with our lives, or this is what could happen. In any case, what it did teach me, is no matter what happens to you or what you do, life will go on. You will probably go through a million changes in life and have not a clue as to why you are going through them, but you must go through them to become the person God wants you to be.

We all went on with our lives and kept shaping ourselves. T, Shea and I never let more than a day go by without at least one of us talking to the other. One conclusion we all came to was, no matter what we did, said, or tried to do in the end, you have to go back to living. You have to go back to life.

About the Author

The author Greg Johnson was born Jan 3rd 1971. From the age of 3, began capturing his family's imagination with elaborate and fantastic stories. From there, Greg Johnson became inspired to write with his musical partner Shannon Harvey while developing and nurturing his passion for rap music and hip-hop culture. After having attended Bakersfield College and Cal St. Hayward University, Greg Johnson developed his writing skills by drawing upon actual events occurring in and around his life and community, cultivating his deepest inspiration from historical, communal, current and spiritual events.

He is the proud father of Amar and Greg Johnson Jr, and currently employed at Powis Parker Inc. as the Shipping and Receiving Manager. During his seven years of employment with them he was awarded employee of the month on many occasions. His dedication to his family, his musical and writing skills, job and artistic passion are what ultimately has led the author to becoming an active contributor to the literary world.